The Tortoise's Tale

- A Novel -

Kendra Coulter

Simon & Schuster

New York   Amsterdam/Antwerp   London
Toronto   Sydney/Melbourne   New Delhi

Simon & Schuster
1230 Avenue of the Americas
New York, NY 10020

For more than 100 years, Simon & Schuster has championed authors and the stories they create. By respecting the copyright of an author's intellectual property, you enable Simon & Schuster and the author to continue publishing exceptional books for years to come. We thank you for supporting the author's copyright by purchasing an authorized edition of this book.

No amount of this book may be reproduced or stored in any format, nor may it be uploaded to any website, database, language-learning model, or other repository, retrieval, or artificial intelligence system without express permission. All rights reserved. Inquiries may be directed to Simon & Schuster, 1230 Avenue of the Americas, New York, NY 10020 or permissions@simonandschuster.com.

This book is a work of fiction. Any references to historical events, real people, or real places are used fictitiously. Other names, characters, places, and events are products of the author's imagination, and any resemblance to actual events or places or persons, living or dead, is entirely coincidental.

Copyright © 2025 by Kendra Coulter

All rights reserved, including the right to reproduce this book or portions thereof in any form whatsoever. For information, address Simon & Schuster Subsidiary Rights Department, 1230 Avenue of the Americas, New York, NY 10020.

First Simon & Schuster hardcover edition November 2025

SIMON & SCHUSTER and colophon are registered trademarks of Simon & Schuster, LLC.

Simon & Schuster strongly believes in freedom of expression and stands against censorship in all its forms. For more information, visit BooksBelong.com.

For information about special discounts for bulk purchases, please contact Simon & Schuster Special Sales at 1-866-506-1949 or business@simonandschuster.com.

The Simon & Schuster Speakers Bureau can bring authors to your live event. For more information or to book an event, contact the Simon & Schuster Speakers Bureau at 1-866-248-3049 or visit our website at www.simonspeakers.com.

Interior design by Ruth Lee-Mui

Manufactured in the United States of America

1 3 5 7 9 10 8 6 4 2

Library of Congress Cataloging-in-Publication Data has been applied for.

ISBN 978-1-6680-6862-5
ISBN 978-1-6680-6864-9 (ebook)

For Jonathan and Fernanda

Who can sing a million songs
Without any words
Patty Griffin

Steadfast

I MISS MUSIC. By no means do I enjoy all of it, let me be perfectly clear about that. But I am something of a musical connoisseur, a nuanced appreciator of your most evocative and rhythmic songs, the uplifting as well as the mournful. Tchaikovsky. Nina Simone. Phil Collins. Shania Twain. Beyoncé. In fact, I have known talented artists personally and been a cherished muse. Sometimes, I imagine that one of them has returned and is singing by the pool as I stand nearby in rapt solidarity and the redbuds glimmer in the moonlight.

Every now and then I feel the ground rumble and think someone is outside. A courageous leader seeking refuge. A compassionate visionary with inspiring plans. A new friend with whom to share a sweet slice of mango as the irrepressible spirit of wonder gently twists around the sharpest points of the cactuses, undaunted.

No visitors arrive. The gates remain closed and the walls solid. I checked them after the smoke finally dissipated and the sky shone again.

Then yesterday, a red-winged blackbird landed on a branch

nearby, and we locked eyes, utterly mesmerized by the sight of another living being. This morning, a pair of blue jays appeared and proceeded to study the place from every angle while I stared, entranced. I want to believe that they are harbingers. Though the vastness of the silence drapes heavily around me, the soft breeze from feathered wings invites a dance of possibility.

You see, I have been given different names: Daisuke, Magic, Shelley, Sara, Zaagi', Fern. Each one is special in its own way. This is my story, but it is not simply about me. Perhaps I am a prism.

Movements

I BEGAN WITH an uncontainable desire for light. Every fiber in my little body was pushing and pulling simultaneously, compelling me to dig and dig and surge upwards. Through incredible determination, I made it to the surface. Once I was quasi-oriented, I saw others like me: minuscule yet mighty. Fetching individuals positively bursting with curiosity. Despite what was surely mutual admiration, we did not feel a need to stay together. Instead, we dispersed and began to explore the symphony of flora and fauna. The shifting sand that had surrounded me was now a steady rhythm beneath my feet. The air swayed in a cooling breeze. The sunbeams sang with promise.

What happened next changed everything. The land was suddenly gone; the air and light too. I was stuffed into a cramped, dark space within which I could barely even wiggle my legs. I sensed the presence of others, their fear rippling out in waves as the distance between our place of birth and our physical location expanded, not because we were moving our own bodies, but because we were being moved. Had there been any warning, we might have been able to assemble and collectively defend ourselves and our right to be left alone, though I suspect that would have been futile. I will neither dwell on the hypothetical, nor suggest that the burden should have fallen to us.

Captivity imposes an overwhelming feeling of loneliness and angst, something I wish on very few individuals, not even the discourteous, selfish, and mocking, whom I detest. As a youngster, I understood nothing of time, so all I can say is that the duration of this indignity remains unknowable. The air became cold, then hot and dry. Those of us who remained were moved again. The light that finally appeared was so bright I could see nothing of my surroundings or captors. I was lifted, prodded by various objects, and ultimately put into a solitary void.

Then it was only me who was taken. I could see nothing at all and heard only some kind of clip-clopping.

When the movement stopped, I was finally liberated from this distressing period of forced immobility but lost and alone. The ground was hard and hot. Enormous palm trees stretched up towards the turquoise sky, and nearby was a small body of water. I marched away from it, seeking the soft richness of soil and grasses under my feet. I proceeded to undertake the exhaustive work of documenting all the details and offerings of this place. I covered significant ground, but there were limits, literal ones. There were walls.

Within them, I relished the many shades of green lyricism, accented by colorful floral punctuation marks. I located all of the coolest spots and sampled plants and flowers from every garden. Equally as important was the identification of the areas I wished to avoid, particularly the giant stone structure that was home to humans. In contrast, I delighted in the fuzzy bees who gracefully moved among the flowers, the rabbits who could shift from still as a tree to quick as a blink, the squirrels who jovially scampered about.

Their presence and welcoming nature brought me comfort as my homeland felt even farther away.

I must have been in this roaming state for many thousands of suns and moons. It did not even occur to me to keep track or to consider time as something to mark. My mind expanded, as did my body, so much so that I became larger than everyone else. One morning, I unexpectedly awakened before dawn and felt the singular need to find a dark and cool quadrant, far from even the slimmest possibility of any prying eyes. I searched for a number of suns with militant focus, reassessing the varied terrains until I was satisfied with a location in the outermost extremity near the back wall that offered particularly fine-grained soil. It was there that I diligently dug a hole into which I placed my first eggs.

This was undoubtedly a significant moment in my own personal development, one indicative of a shift from youth into something more mature, though not what I would call maturity by any means. But this egg-creating-and-laying process seemed normal, a new addition to my comings and goings. I promptly moved on, feeling no need to remain in place, and returned to one of my preferred shaded areas where I could dine peacefully with minimal risk of human interruption.

Back then, I would simply retreat into the thickest green spaces whenever people's noise levels increased—that is, until I heard the wild assemblage of instrumentation that is jazz. It was the very first time I had encountered music not made by birds, and its mysterious sounds were enticing. Despite the rather substantial quantity of terrain I had to traverse, I set off in the direction of the music's source. The sound came more into focus as I approached, adding to my enchantment. I was trying to muster the courage to get even closer when the music fell silent and all that remained was the rubble of the party in the distance and the soft light of the moon.

Despite my commitment to avoiding human interaction, I made a bold and earnest decision to enter a lush garden adjacent to the pool and linger there with the utmost discretion, hoping for the music to return. After many moons of silence, I took leave and reimmersed myself in the avian melodies.

The sonic mélange of jazz returned, what must have been hundreds of suns later, and I promptly embarked on another quixotic journey towards it. Once again, I did not make it close enough to observe anything of value visually, but I was able to hear more clearly. The music was energizing and lively. In fact, I believed it was being created here, by people. After that, I began to hear faint melodies emanating from inside the human residence more frequently. That was vivacious, big band music, yet even then I discerned that it sounded trapped, as if being boxed in. The music needed to stretch and surge out into the night air.

Thankfully, there was a continuous rainbow of birds whose enlivening harmonies brought cherished vibrancy. Most were free to come and go as they pleased, but I discovered that some poor souls had been confined to cages located in the outer vicinity of the pool. I felt their longing for freedom in all the caverns of my heart.

I stood near the caged birds as much as I could to bring them comfort. I would close my eyes and allow their music to envelop me. First, their dawn chorus, still celebrating the beginning of a new day, despite their captivity. Then their reassuring or perhaps somber refrains, shared and returned. "We are here." "We are here."

"We are still here."

Ralph became a person I could not entirely avoid, the first proprietor who wandered (somewhat) farther out into the landscapes beyond the concrete, always sporting impeccably tailored suits. Among his varied activities, he would periodically emerge from the residence to provide seeds for these birds.

"Good day, old chap," he would say, tossing some in my direction, although I was neither old nor a chap. The seed was far from my favorite, but I would partake nevertheless.

Early in Ralph's tenure, I heard a party outdoors complete with music. I was not a great distance away from the pool area and became determined to get as close as possible with the intention of seeing but not being seen. I was able to achieve this goal and yet observed no live musicians. The music was emerging from what I then naively understood to be simply an elaborate box. How I longed to hear a big band up close, or a small band, really any sized band.

This music still summoned me, and I was so focused on listening and getting closer to the sound that I wandered into plain view. My presence was noticed and caused something of a scene. Then I was lifted. I retreated into myself with a hiss and was returned to the ground with moderate gentleness. No one bothered me further on that occasion. I realized that I could, under the correct circumstances and with sufficient strategizing, place myself closer to people and not face a litany of unwelcome interactions. I began to cautiously linger during parties, which were hosted more than ever before. The music varied and often included lovely vocal harmonies accompanied by a light, boppy sound. A popular tune was especially pleasing, and though I could not entirely decipher its words given my cursory level of education at the time, I believe it was about a sandman who brings slumber, an excellent topic indeed.

Yet as time passed, people seemed to become more emboldened. If noticed, invariably I would be lifted and someone would feel both compelled and entitled to poke me, often right on my nose if not retreated. I would then be abandoned once again, allowed to resume my movements at a pace and purpose of my own choosing or to simply remain in peace. As a result, I attempted to find locations that would allow me to listen but not be bothered. It was a challenging balancing act. The cage area often offered the best prospects, and I spent many suns and moons there whether a party was taking place or not, because there was always the music of the trapped birds.

The cluster of cages became a cacophony when Ralph arrived with a monkey who wailed through the night. I had to take leave from the area at that point as it was simply too heartbreaking. The second moon I took shelter near a sculptured pond with rigid sides and delicious water. Sadly, I could still hear Monkey, whose cries would come in bursts and then subside, only to return, a melancholy ballad of imprisonment.

When the dark blue tendrils of the dawn emerged and most of the sorrow silenced, I stretched my head and neck, stood up, and moved towards the pond. I would not normally rise so early, but this was an atypical time. One of the buoyant pink flowers had drifted to the edge, right into perfect snacking range. I reached for it but was interrupted. The sound of a groan accompanied the feeling of being partly lifted and somewhat dragged. Takeo had returned. We had coexisted but not directly interacted, this man and I. He was never impolite, so I did not retreat from his presence, yet I rarely found myself near him for long given his busy schedule tending to the gardens.

"Omoi," he said, straining to place me in nearby shade before returning to the pond and sliding the elusive snack back to the center, out of reach, and ever so gently stirring the water.

I kept an eye on him as the violet waves of the sky transformed into beaming orange, and the heat somehow both rose up and descended. Monkey cried, but less often. Takeo came and went with his shears and hoe. I dug a shallow hole in the cool soil and tucked into myself to rest. I had drifted off into light slumber when a soft fragrance enticed me to awaken. In front of me was a cherished item, one as beautiful as it is delicious: the magenta flower of the prickly pear cactus.

"Kyoryoku shitekurete arigatō," Takeo said to thank me for not dining on his lilies, offering me the bud instead. I graciously accepted, savoring the flavor while chewing voraciously. I did not care for being moved or denied the floating treat, but Takeo had provided me with a suitable alternative, and I appreciated that gesture. He seemed to understand my sophisticated palate.

That was a turning point for Takeo and me. I began to watch him work, most effectively when he remained in a specific region and moved less quickly to and fro. Takeo would rarely take breaks, but on some occasions, he would find me and sit nearby for a few fleeting moments. When logistically possible, I would position myself beside a bench or somewhere similarly suitable with shade nearby to make it easier for him. Some days he had no time to rest and had to swiftly move off to tend to a different cluster of hedges or the flowers that needed far more to drink than these lands and the sky provided. Flowers that, like me, had been taken from somewhere else and expected to survive here. Even then, people knew the flowers needed extra care as a result of their transfer.

I learned that for Takeo, this daily toil was about beauty and pride. I understood the amount of sweat he had poured into that pond where I had first tried to sneak a lily, that his blood fertilized every garden. He truly cared for this land and its inhabitants, far more than Ralph did, early proof that ownership is not always synonymous with genuine affection or duty. Takeo would share the fruits of his labor and not deny me culinary pleasures, but there were certain exceptions. I honored his requests because I witnessed his devotion; even when he cut, it was done deliberately, to help sustain life, not take it away. He was a garden artist.

I learned a little bit of Japanese but not enough. One word was monumental: Daisuke. He would often start a sentence with the word, or end with it, and its meaning became clear. I was Daisuke. It was his name for me. This was the first time a person saw me and understood that I am someone.

On what seemed like an ordinary morning, I spotted Takeo in one of the gardens near the cages. He was adding little trees that looked like puffs on stilts and were not the least bit appetizing, but this was his assignment, and I would support him. The birds were in their daily recognition chorus. Monkey was silent and still, slumped in the back corner. I closed my eyes in anger as I passed.

A woman and man from the residence were outside by the pool. They went back inside, then the woman returned. By the time I arrived in the vicinity, she was gone again.

"Ohayō, Daisuke," Takeo said when he saw me. Along with the stilt puffs, he was planting a blanket of tiny, delicate purple flowers.

The woman reemerged with two others. It became clear what was going on: They were setting up for a party. Due to my evolving grandeur, even if I was spotted during an evening of frivolity, the lift-poke was happening less often, and I felt comfortable remaining near the cages. Because the truth is that there was some good that came from Ralph's festivities, beyond the music. They introduced me to human laughter. Laughter was different from words; that I knew right away despite my then elementary grasp of the English language. Laughter was more melodic. I enjoyed it, although I still generally preferred to be on my own or near only Takeo. Yet this particular party was my introduction to something else, one of the central contradictions of human life, in fact. The very same acts that bring enjoyment to some can cause pain to others.

I watched from a safe distance under green cover near the cages as people arrived. Guests lingered in pairs or trios. Some formed a circle around Ralph and laughed a great deal at his antics. One woman in particular spent a lot of time near him. The music got louder, and people danced. It was an unusual sound, markedly different from the typically smooth songs Ralph would play by the pool. This music brought a more raucous sound I came to learn was rockabilly, a genre I quite enjoy.

A group of frolickers broke off and wandered towards the cages. Regrettably, a man noticed me and marched right in my direction. His comportment and overall demeanor signaled pending disrespect, and I swiftly pulled into myself. He tried, unsuccessfully of course, to lift me, so recruited a partner in crime. They managed to hoist me and proceeded to run around in circles as others laughed. This was not laughter I liked, not one bit. Laughter is not pleasant when the reason for it is unadmirable.

They set me down with a thud when they realized the women in this splinter group were now watching Monkey, who was huddled in the back corner. The men went right up to the bars and reached through, trying to draw Monkey forward with words and gestures. The birds, interrupted from their slumber by the tomfoolery, sang strange notes I had not heard before.

"Just leave it," one of the women said.

Monkey was a she, not an it, but I appreciated the intention behind the statement nevertheless.

Yet the men kept trying to lure Monkey. One rolled a bottle into the cage, its contents pouring out on the ground. Monkey somehow inched farther back.

The women retreated, making their way back towards the pool, and mercifully the two men followed. Ralph noticed his guests who had wandered and said something funny to the women, then joined the men. They rubbed their crotches in a most undignified manner on the stilt-puff trees, finding all of this hilarious, indifferent to the fact that they were stomping all over Takeo's delicate purple flower bed. Even Ralph stepped carelessly, without any regard for the damage he was doing. I closed my eyes to escape from it all.

The next morning, Takeo's face betrayed no emotion when he saw the state of his fledgling petals. He salvaged those he could, replanting them gently and supplementing the gaps left by those he could not save with an assortment of simple green choices, their appeal different from the intended violet tapestry but still lovely, in my view.

Takeo was examining the results of his repair work when an unusual sound extended from the island of cages. Monkey was rolling the glass bottle along the ground, back and forth, back and forth.

"Sore wa abunai," Takeo said, noting the risk of what Monkey was doing, as he strained to reach the bottle and remove it. Monkey sat down in the back corner.

Takeo did not join me midday when he would normally tend to his own sustenance. I hypothesized that he might have sought complete solitude to process the flippant disregard for his garden that had taken place the night before. He had responded with stoicism upon seeing the destruction, but this was undoubtedly a well-worn mask. As the sun was beginning its journey west, Takeo reappeared carrying a blue ball. He squeezed it through the bars and gently pushed it towards Monkey.

Monkey did not approach the ball at first, but instead studied the scenario and Takeo, who sat down in the shade on the ground near me. Monkey gingerly moved towards the ball. At first, she tested to see if it was edible. Then, realizing that this item was not for eating but rather for playing, she began to roll the ball along the concrete. She gently bounced it against the wall and watched the ball roll back. I heard a sound I had not heard before, but thankfully, it was one I heard more often thereafter. A simple chord of joy.

The ball was not a friend. It was not a family. It was not Monkey's homeland, or freedom, or anything resembling a normal life. But it was something. It was a small gift, "chottoshita okurimono." Takeo was smiling. He even laughed.

A Spot of Magic

ONE MORNING I was making my way towards the cages, now finding that area somewhat less woeful yet still in need of my unwavering support, when I heard a distinct and almost guttural yell slicing through the trees. It was behind me, then it was gone. Back again in the direction of Takeo's favorite pond. Next a long, impolite call extending along the path to the cages and pool.

"Emmet, please stop being so loud."

This was a voice the likes of which I had never heard before. It was gentle but far from hollow—musical, really. I began to turn myself around so I could see its source.

"Scram," Emmet shouted as he suddenly appeared, tearing along with a plane in hand.

"Oh, let him play, Lucy," a woman said.

Lucy shone like a ray of sunshine. She was even smaller than Emmet and wearing a yellow dress.

"Don't linger out here too long. Uncle Ralph will be home for dinner." The woman retreated in the direction of the residence.

Lucy walked towards the cages. She did not get too close and simply studied the birds, her face revealing a mixture of curiosity and concern. I began to approach. She moved around to the side, having noticed Monkey, who was peering back at her.

"Hello there, little one. Are you okay?"

Someone called for her and Emmet from the house. Lucy said goodbye to Monkey and the birds, then was gone.

How I wanted her to stay, to see me too.

Thinking and hoping she would return, I moved under a cluster of nearby bushes, planning to emerge and march towards her in a grandiose manner. However, only Emmet reappeared that evening, unaccompanied, and there was neither sign nor sound of Lucy. He still had the plane and proceeded to noisily fly it around, crashing through various gardens and jumping over hedges. The free birds took leave, choosing to settle elsewhere in preparation for the moon's arrival, somewhere with less disruption, undoubtedly.

From inside myself, I could see part of Emmet's face. He began poking me with a stick! Thankfully, he quickly lost interest, and I opted to move farther away from the cages as a precautionary measure.

The next morning, I again hid when I heard his bluster. He zoomed past me, and I thought I was home free, but then I was struck by something from the side. It was a rock. Admittedly more of a small stone, but Emmet had thrown it right at me. It happened again. I had done absolutely nothing to deserve this barrage.

"Hello." It was Takeo. He seemed to be trying to distract the boy and spare me from this shameful display.

"Hello," Emmet replied, rather curtly.

"Will you swim in the pool?" Takeo asked. "It is going to be a very hot day."

"Oh, probably. I'm a good swimmer. My grandfather has a pool."

"Ah. Well, I wish you a pleasant day," Takeo said.

Emmet said nothing further, but the rock tossing also stopped. I peeked my head out tentatively and he was nowhere to be seen.

The following sun, I awoke to hear Emmet bustling around the pool. A second voice. My heart skipped a beat. But the other voice belonged to another boy. I feared the pair of them would create a tag team of knocking or stone hurtling or poking.

In the distance, I spotted Takeo, who was working near the most heavily wooded area, something he did infrequently because it was a more self-sustaining quadrant, the flora and foliage hardy and dense, as if closing ranks. I was all but certain that Takeo would be long gone by the time I arrived, but I made my way to the green mosaic nevertheless, feeling drawn to its coy mystery and comfortable putting distance between myself and the rowdy boys.

When I finally reached the outskirts of the forest, there was a creaking sound emerging from within the trees, one I had heard only once before when a fierce storm made the branches teeter and waver erratically. Now, this creak continued steadily like a metronome rooted in the mossy ground. Through the canopy I saw movement, a flash of green, lighter than any plants or grasses in this place. Then as soon as it appeared, it was gone again, only to reappear, perfectly in sync with the rhythm. I moved into the forest, something I had not done since I was a much smaller version of myself. As I crossed the wooden threshold, it became clear that Takeo had been collecting and removing fallen branches to expose a smooth pathway. There are rare instances when timing is perfectly aligned, and this was one such symbiosis.

The sound got louder as I made my way down the path, and the pale green again flashed before me.

"Oh my goodness," I heard. The voice was unmistakable. It was Lucy!

She was seated on a wooden swing and sailing through the air like a hummingbird. She slowed, disembarked, and approached me. I stopped in my tracks, hopeful but still unsure, and accustomed to humans failing to maintain even a modicum of personal space when they first encountered me.

"Hello," she said. "It's a pleasure to make your acquaintance." She looked right into my eyes and I held her gaze. She walked all the way around me but did not get too close. "Well, aren't you gorgeous."

My heart fluttered like a butterfly.

Despite the gentle mightiness of her voice, Lucy was really quite a tiny human, only a neck taller than me. She sat down on a log, and I dare say we became nearly identical in height, twins almost. A robin chirped nearby and caught her attention. She watched the bird forage in the soil and then looked back to me, smiling. I hoped this time would stretch out like the sky.

"I love it in here," she said. "It's so peaceful."

It certainly was. The trees provided protection from the sounds of the occasional engine erupting from out of view, and from the unwanted interventions of, ahem, certain people within the walls.

"Were you here before Uncle Ralph? I want to ask him, but part of me doesn't want him to know I met you." She studied me some more, her little head tilting. "Where are you from?"

How I longed to tell her my memories and to hear about her. Where she was from. What she liked to do, besides basking in the beauty of this place. Would she be staying?

Muffled sound broke through the shield of the trees.

"Lucy!"

The summoning voice was, thankfully, quite a distance away. Our hideout would not be discovered, at least not yet, and could remain a sanctuary.

"I suppose I must go, but I will return tomorrow. I hope we

meet again." She stood up and dusted twigs off her dress. She placed her finger to her lips. "Let's keep this our little secret."

She had my word.

Feeling empowered, I remained in the forest as darkness arrived, my legs buried in some wonderful cool soil. A mouse ran over me as they made their way along, the flurry of tiny footsteps a soft vibration gone as soon as it arrived. A rabbit stealthily appeared nearby, had a bite to eat, and then hopped off into the darkness. The night birds awakened by the moon provided a lullaby. I slept comfortably, buoyed by the remarkable events that had just transpired.

It was not until the sun was at its highest peak that Lucy returned. I had held firm, exactly where she had left me, to ensure I would be easy to find.

"Hello again!" she said. "I'm afraid I can't stay long. It seems my vacation is all but over."

I had only just met her and now she was leaving? This was a catastrophe.

"It's a good thing, though. Emmet's tutor is coming."

I did not have the necessary context for understanding this news. I knew little of the comings and goings of the residence, or what Ralph did, let alone the particulars of Lucy's family other than the noisiness of her brother and the presence of her mother, who seemed to always be limiting her daughter's time outdoors and interrupting at the most inopportune times. Normally this ignorance was of no bother. But now that I had met Lucy, I yearned for more knowledge and understanding.

"Right now, we have this time, so let's enjoy it," she said. By *enjoyment*, she meant exploration, quiet reflection, observation, and appreciation, all superb choices. She looked up, admiring a host of sparrows, and down at the forest floor as a caterpillar gently strolled along. A squirrel scurried behind a tree, then peeked back out before hurrying onwards with their journey. The rabbit reappeared not far from us, one ear forward and the other back, listening.

"Oh, I feel like Alice!" Lucy said. I was unsure of who Alice was but thought that if she was anything like Lucy, I would most enjoy meeting her too. The rabbit stood up on their hind legs, looking regal indeed. They sniffed the air and then opted to move off.

"Should we follow?" Lucy asked me. "No, I think we would startle the rabbit if we did that."

She sat right down on the ground.

"This has been a magical time. I think that's what I will call you: Magic."

Lucy had given me my second name!

Charmed

A VERITABLE MIXTURE of curiosity and glee flowed through me when I emerged from the forest. While my connection with Takeo was one of calm and steady rootedness, Lucy filled me with effervescence. She was the smallest person I had ever seen and yet she was bursting with enough light for someone three times her size. I needed to find out as much about her as I could, so began making my way to the pool. I estimated that if I proceeded directly, briskly, and without delay (that is, by forgoing naps completely), I could arrive with enough time before sundown to choose a strategic vantage point and get settled in. There might be happenings in the golden hour or even early darkness, and if not, I would be ready for the rising of the sun and this momentous arrival of Emmet's tutor.

"Kekkona tabi da, Daisuke," Takeo said as he walked by. I *was* on quite a journey. He plucked a white flower from an adjacent garden for me and I relished this tasty offering.

My prediction was correct, and I arrived near the pool as the sun descended and its golden light radiated through the sky, illuminating this place with a soft glow. I ensconced myself near one of the smaller buildings to rest after the extensive travel. Ralph was seated at a poolside table in conversation with another man. Emmet was playing with small toy vehicles. Lucy was not outside. It all seemed very ordinary, until suddenly a man walked out with Lucy's mother, first to Ralph for a quick exchange of pleasantries and then over to Emmet.

"Good evening, Emmet. I am Mr. Williams. It is a pleasure to meet you," he said, stretching out his hand. He dressed like Ralph and spoke the same words, but the cadence was different, the pronunciation. This was the first time I had heard a British accent.

Mother stared at Emmet, who then pulled himself onto his feet and shook Mr. Williams's hand but remained silent.

"Emmet, please," Mother said.

"It's a pleasure to meet you too, sir," Emmet replied.

"I am most looking forward to our time together," Mr. Williams said. "And what a beautiful place to spend it in. Such exquisite gardens."

Emmet simply shrugged. I was aghast at his listless response.

"I think we shall have our lessons out here, in fact, if that is all right with you, Mrs. Harrington."

"I don't think that will be a problem. We are here for sun and fresh air, after all."

"Fresh air you shall have! Along with the highest quality education. What a wonderful combination."

The boy again shrugged.

Mother guided Mr. Williams not towards the residence but rather in the direction of a smaller house whose surrounding soils I had walked through only once or maybe twice. Darkness began to descend, and Mother reappeared to usher Emmet back inside, while Ralph and his guest remained. I tucked into myself, deeming my current location suitable for slumber and ideal for surveying the activities that would surely transpire once the sun reemerged.

Lucy was still nowhere to be seen.

• • •

I was in such a state of anxious excitement that the indigo waves of dawn lifted my eyelids. There was some activity near the residence, but nothing atypical, and the pool area was calm. The pool-tending man arrived, brushed the water, then went on his way. Mr. Williams arrived alone and set up in the shade of a cabana beside the pool, with walls on either side but its front and back open to the air. From within his bag, he removed a globe and various papers. Then he sat at the table and waited. He read through the papers. He stood up and took a little stroll around the closest garden, glancing at the main residence periodically.

Around the corner, Lucy was leaning up against the wall. Mr. Williams noticed her, too, and wandered over.

"Good morning, young lady."

"Good morning, sir."

"And who might you be?"

"Lucy Harrington, sir. It's a pleasure to make your acquaintance." She dipped slightly in a curtsy.

"Goodness, Miss Lucy, you are most charming, but there really is no need to bow for me. I am not royalty and the pleasure is mine. Do you live here or are you just visiting?"

"Mmm, somewhere in between. We are visiting my uncle Ralph, but I don't know how long we're staying, exactly. They don't always tell me things, you see. I have my ways, though."

Mr. Williams laughed. I was envious that he was able to converse with her, and desperately wanted to join, but felt compelled to stay where I was, unnoticed, at least until I figured out exactly what was going on.

"So, Mr. Emmet is your brother, is he?"

"Yes. I'm nearly as old as he is."

"He is a bit tardy this morning. Do you happen to know where he might be?"

Lucy shook her head. "I think he's simply late. He's not very punctual."

"Will you be joining us for lessons, then?"

Lucy's face changed, ever so slightly. A less refined observer might have missed it, but not I.

"I'm not able to join you, Mr. Williams. You are here for Emmet."

Her mouth opened to say more, but the discussion was interrupted by the arrival of Emmet, being hurried along by Mother, who ushered him right into the chair that was waiting. Lucy snuck off with alacrity.

"Our sincerest apologies, Mr. Williams," Mother said.

"Not at all. I am most delighted to see you and was simply—" He turned and realized that Lucy had vanished during the commotion. "Well, let us get started, then, shall we?"

And that they did. Mr. Williams began by teaching Emmet writing and grammar, but through stories of adventure. He would point to somewhere on the globe and then delve into a lesson. Emmet seemed less than enthused but became more energized when Mr. Williams started incorporating modes of transportation into the setups: automobiles, airplanes, trains. I followed along with razor-sharp focus, absorbing everything. The earth was a marvel! This education was exactly what I needed to take my understanding of human language and those who speak it beyond the basic level I had cobbled together from observational study, which skewed heavily to the business of railroads and party banter as a result. I longed to reach the peaks of comprehension and eloquence, something that now seemed well within my reach thanks to the arrival of Mr. Williams and the pedagogical methods he was employing.

I also stared at that globe and wondered where my homeland was located.

When one of the women from the house arrived with light refreshments, Mr. Williams took a break, pausing a riveting lesson about apostrophes. It was then that I realized Lucy had returned. She was again around the corner, now sitting on the hard ground, out of view. Lucy continued to lean against the wall, listening, until the children were called in for lunch. She circled around, presumably to create the impression that she had not been there all along.

I understood so much more about English vocabulary and geography already, but none of it helped me make sense of the art and science of little girls and why Lucy couldn't join the lessons. The human world is far more complicated than grammar.

I contemplated retreating to the greenery near the cages to ensure that the imprisoned birds and Monkey were well, or as well as they could be given the conditions of their current existence. But the intensity of focus required for the structured lessons had worn me out and I nodded off.

I was awakened by the sound of plates clinking to find that dinner would be served to both adult and child guests by the pool on this occasion, a boy and two parents. Ralph drank with gusto and conversed with the man about the leadership of someone they both knew named Dwight and a peculiar "race" that involved space (I pieced together its meaning in more detail over time and with significant intellectual labor due to the strangeness of the entire endeavor).

"Lucy, please eat your steak," Mother said.

"No, thank you," Lucy replied.

"Sweetheart," Mother said, her voice calm but firm.

"I'm enjoying the bread and vegetables, thank you."

"I'll eat it if she doesn't want it," Emmet said.

"Me too," the other boy said.

"You are welcome to more, Al," Mother said.

"Our Nancy is the same now," the woman said to Mother but quietly. "Emmet, I hear you had a busy day of lessons? How was that?"

"It was all right."

"Will you be attending school here in the fall?"

"Apparently," Emmet replied, clearly annoyed.

I felt quite the opposite. What news!

"Aw, come on, pal." This was Ralph. "There's lots to love about California. How can you beat this weather?"

"May I please be excused?" Lucy asked.

"Last one to the fountain has to drink from it!" Emmet said, pushing his chair back, and the two boys took off running towards the far side of the residence. (This fountain was of no use to me, by the way. I could not climb its hefty stone base to access the thirst-quenching riches that soared up to the sky and returned simultaneously. As a result, after my initial assessment, I simply avoided it.)

Lucy took her notebook to one of the longer chairs farther down the length of the pool. The adults kept talking and drinking. Ralph continued to entertain and inspire bouts of laughter. As the sun descended, its late-day golden glow was replaced by the soft gray of dusk. Lights around the pool shimmered, their rays bouncing off the water, which swayed gently in the breeze. The crickets provided the first evening songs. It was beautiful—there was no doubt about that—and I delighted in the knowledge that I would have many more moons and suns of Lucy's melodies too.

Lessons of a Higher Order

THE FOLLOWING SUN brought grave heat. Mr. Williams and Emmet were back in action while Lucy was, once again, discreetly positioned around the corner against the wall. I kept pace with the lessons, but the intensity of the temperature surged through my body. I felt dulled, even in the shade. Takeo was behind the teaching area watering gardens with the hose. The hose! I had to act. Although my top pace requires additional exertion of energy and thus tires me, I needed to get myself to Takeo before he moved on. It was a risk, but one I simply had to take given the distressing conditions and their regrettable impact on my learning. The most direct route allowed me to travel while remaining within hearing range of Mr. Williams. I desperately tried to listen while I marched but heard only bits and bobs.

"Ohayō, Daisuke," Takeo said, spotting me.

At this point, I had to abandon the lesson and focus entirely on my destination. I concentrated on each leg and its propulsion, trying to ignore the heat of the concrete as I left the grass. I felt moist soil next as I stepped into the garden, and it brought tender comfort and renewed promise. I maintained my momentum towards Takeo. As I got closer, I felt tiny droplets first, a rush of sweet, sweet relief. Takeo seemed to understand exactly what I was doing and walked closer with the hose, sparing me further travel.

He proceeded to spray my whole body with water. It was absolutely glorious. A small pool formed at my feet, and I lay down, enveloped by its refreshing splendor. The mist tickled my face.

"Good day," Mr. Williams said tentatively. He was standing at the edge of the garden. Emmet was no longer at the table. Admittedly, I knew little of what had transpired in the learning area during the harrowing journey that demanded both my physical and intellectual attention.

"Good morning, sir," Takeo replied.

"A very good morning to you too. This creature, it is magnificent."

I was not an it but was otherwise flattered.

Takeo nodded. "Yes, sir."

"Does it just roam about as it pleases?"

Takeo kept the hose on me as he spoke. "Yes. He has favorite places."

Takeo thought I was a he—preferable to being an it, undoubtedly, and a forgivable mistake. I always laid my eggs alone and well out of sight, far away from even the lowest maintenance sections that only periodically received visits from Takeo. Most significantly, I was delighted that Takeo knew I had preferences. Moreover, not only did he know, but he shared this important information with someone as significant as the teacher.

"Do you think it could join my lessons over there?"

Takeo looked unsure. He hesitated before saying, "I think so."

"Right, well, then how could we do that? It would be a folly to assume it comes when it is called. Am I correct in that assertion?" Mr. Williams chuckled.

I did not know what to think. I buried down into the now wet pool of soil that surrounded me, relishing every descending degree as I dug my legs farther under the ground.

"Might you have some sort of useful item, like a—goodness, well, what is it we would need?"

Takeo did not immediately reply. He was still uncertain. For my part, now that I had returned to a proper temperature, I was able to think more clearly.

Mr. Williams wanted me in his poolside classroom. But why? I could not imagine he meant me harm. Mr. Williams seemed to be the embodiment of good manners. I now know that politeness can be a disguise for many shades of unpleasantness and disloyalty, treachery even. But at this particular moment, as I lay comfortably in the refreshing mud, I was simply soaked in uncertainty about why Mr. Williams sought my presence in his educational offerings. Nevertheless, I saw potential in his proposition. Given that I had been learning a great deal from my secret lookout, how much more could I learn in direct proximity to the lessons? That prospect enlivened me.

"A wheelbarrow? Yes, perhaps a wheelbarrow," Mr. Williams suggested.

Was I to be wheeled about? I must admit that while initially I was ambivalent, I promptly became enthusiastic about this possibility. In the wrong hands, such technology could lead to no end of difficulties for me; of that I was certain. Yet I felt confident that Takeo would drive me in style and with great care.

This process turned into something of a production. Takeo, upon fetching the wheelbarrow, realized that I had become far too heavy for him to even begin to lift on his own. He had to enlist the pool-cleaning man, who had been somewhere near the residence, out of view. Together, and with not insignificant effort, they hoisted me into the chariot.

At first, the sensation of being moved brought back visceral memories from my earliest days, and I remembered the even-more-harrowing journey that began in my homeland and ultimately concluded with me here. This sensory recollection was unsettling, but I focused on the present, on this revelatory new chapter, which had the potential to transform me from secret observer at a distance to direct witness right in the heart of the educational endeavor . . . or even, could it possibly be? Participant? The possibility tingled through my body. Simultaneously, the experience of being driven by Takeo was splendid. The view from this different pace and unique vantage point was lovely, and I appreciated the complete lack of effort required from me. I might have enjoyed quite a tour about the place had the promise of the classroom not been so tempting.

"I think right about here would be perfect," Mr. Williams said, gesturing to a location directly adjacent to the table.

"One, two, three." Takeo and Pool-Cleaning Man hoisted me on three and placed me gingerly on the ground. The process proceeded in a highly pleasing fashion.

"Ah yes, that is lovely. Thank you, sirs," Mr. Williams said. Pool-Cleaning Man departed with a nod, heading back in the direction of the residence.

"Do you think it will stay put?" Mr. Williams asked Takeo.

"Maybe," he replied with a smile as he began to drive the now empty wheelbarrow away.

Mr. Williams studied me some more before saying "Right, then" to no one in particular, checking his wristwatch, and sitting down. He began reading, so missed what happened next, but I, most certainly, was privy to it. A tiny face peered around the corner closest to the pool. Lucy was examining what had transpired. Her mouth opened in a silent gasp when she saw me, and then she vanished.

Emmet returned from the residence, meandering as he walked.

"Mr. Emmet, look at what we have here," Mr. Williams said.

"Yeah, I've seen it before," Emmet replied, but the dismissive words were contradicted by a little smile. He sat down but kept glancing over at me.

"Do you know what this is?" Mr. Williams asked.

"A really big turtle?"

"Close. If I am not mistaken, this is a tortoise, specifically. It has a most unusual spelling . . ."

Tortoise. I was a tortoise! A tortoise. *Tor-toise*. What a perfect word. I could not have come up with something better myself. After allowing this insight to permeate my mind, I longed to know more. What was the name of the tortoise homeland? Where were the other tortoises? Would any more tortoises be brought here? These questions flowed through me as Emmet practiced the spelling of *tortoise*, and a soft breeze arrived, bringing with it a wave of delightfully cooler air and possibility.

"What do people do with tortoises?" Emmet asked.

Mr. Williams paused. Perhaps this boy was testing the limits of his teacher's knowledge. Nevertheless, I waited with bated breath, hoping for an answer.

"Well, Mr. Emmet, I think mostly people eat them."

The face Emmet made barely scratched the surface of the depth of dismay and disgust that rose up from me. People eat tortoises?

I am a tortoise.

Were people going to eat me?

My elation at having become integrated into the lesson began to seep away. Was this what deeper knowledge brought? Word of my demise? Advanced notice of my fallibility? A potent cocktail of emotion surged through me, but the dominant flavors were confusion and fury. I had resided in this place since I was barely bigger than the ball Monkey played with. I had been here well, well before any of these people. If they were going to eat me, what were they waiting for? More to the point, how would they do so? They needed two men and a wheelbarrow to move me, for goodness' sake.

"People eat that?" Emmet said, pointing. He was alternating between looking at Mr. Williams and at me. Maybe he was asking himself the very same questions. New queries filled my mind. Serious inquiries. Should I flee? Do I need to get away from these people? From all people? Am I in mortal danger at this very moment? In every moment?

"Well, not most people, no. We certainly will not be eating the tortoise. I think primarily sailors on long journeys. I admit, my knowledge of tortoises could be greater. What I do know is that there is a second animal with a similar spelling. Do you know what animal that is?"

Emmet shook his head.

"Porpoise. Shall we spell *porpoise*?"

As interesting as these porpoise creatures must be, my mind remained focused on the other significant information. Most people did not eat tortoises. This was a crucial fact. I would watch out for these so-called sailors.

"It's a table," Emmet said, jumping up. He grabbed his plane and moved directly towards me. I retreated posthaste and felt him place the item on my back.

I remained inside myself as the lesson recommenced. In the span of mere human minutes, I had been granted access to the core of my identity, a fundamental truth about who I am. Were there other tortoises, beyond these walls, who had not been eaten? Surely, some had to have escaped. While we had been futile in the face of those who had removed us from the sands of our birthplace, there must have been others, in the same area or nearby, who had successfully resisted or otherwise remained uncaptured. They may have been able to retreat, to hide, to blend in among whatever foliage is in our homeland and thus survive. I felt it to be true . . . I hoped it was true.

Then I began to wonder why I had survived. What was it about me? I had been taken and moved, like so many others. What had become of those who had been stacked above and below me? Was I different somehow? It was not right that I should be alive if others were not. Or was it simply luck? Such significant matters should not be dependent on mere chance. All of this pained me.

I emerged tentatively from inside myself. The remaining lesson had changed topics completely and was now about numbers, which were of less interest. This was a minor blessing because I was unable to properly concentrate. I needed to dedicate my intellect to processing what had transpired. It was then that I realized the full implications of being part of the educational endeavor. The truth can be complicated, disquieting, or even ugly. Sometimes, the truth hurts.

"You're a pretty good table," Emmet said as he got up and walked in my direction once again. I lacked the will to retreat and resigned myself to the likelihood of poking. Instead, he simply collected his plane from my back and ran off.

Mr. Williams smiled at me as he departed. I considered moving myself to somewhere more private but was unable to muster the energy and fell into sleep.

The next thing I remember was the soft and celebratory sound of the free birds' chorus rising up from the trees, coinciding with the reemergence of the sun, a gentler incarnation with less ferocity. As I stretched my neck forward, I noticed an unexpected delivery. There, directly in front of me, was a delicious white flower I called heavenly trumpet. And alongside it, a slice of orange. I had never before been offered such an item. Its sweet juices enveloped my tongue in decadence. This was a most generous gesture on the part of whoever had selected and provided these gifts for me.

Many questions and uncertainties lingered, but I had a unique opportunity. A duty, in fact. I had to learn more, as much as possible. I was ready to face whatever was in store, as Daisuke and Magic, and as a tortoise.

A Path to Independence

I WAS AGAIN made into a table, albeit not literally.

"Let us begin with some review to ease gently into our work today. Do you use *a* or *an* before words beginning with the letter *h*?" Mr. Williams asked.

Emmet was silent. His eyes wandered to the item he had placed on me.

"Think back, Mr. Emmet. I am confident this rule of grammar is residing comfortably in your memory. Reflect on time and its passage, in fact, as a memory aid."

Nothing from Emmet.

"Well then, what do you think, Miss Lucy?" Mr. Williams said, at a louder volume.

Silence. Emmet looked around.

"I would welcome even a guess," Mr. Williams said again at a pitch decidedly not intended for someone sitting directly beside him.

From around the corner, the wee human appeared, revealing herself. She was in the same light green dress she had been wearing on that delightful day when we first properly made our acquaintance in the forest sanctuary.

"Good morning," she said quietly.

"Good morning. Do you know the answer?"

"You use *an* before words beginning with *h* when the *h* is silent. For example, not *a hour*, but rather *an hour*."

"That is correct, Miss Harrington. Do you wish to join us on this lovely day?"

Lucy looked at her brother, then at me, but said nothing.

"Surely you would be more comfortable here than seated on the ground?"

Mr. Williams knew of her attempted covert operation. How long he had known, I could not be sure. Lucy's face turned a delicate shade of pink. I believe embarrassment is a distinctly human feeling and am certain I have experienced nothing of the sort. Though I have also observed people who should feel embarrassed yet do not.

"We could easily find another chair for you; I am most confident of that."

"I'm not supposed to be here."

"Where is it that you are supposed to be, exactly?"

"I don't think it matters."

"Then, what are you supposed to be doing?"

"Nothing."

"You are supposed to be doing nothing?"

Lucy shrugged. "Well, I mean, nothing in particular is set up for me. It's fine if I do nothing."

"Yet you are not supposed to be at your brother's lessons?"

"I asked."

"What did you ask?"

"I asked if I could have lessons. They said no and that there would be time later for me to learn what I needed to learn."

"Yet you have been sitting on the ground for how many days now, nevertheless."

Lucy's face flushed pink once again.

"Young Mr. Harrington, would you object terribly if your sister joined in the lessons? Or perhaps some of the lessons if she finds she has other engagements?"

"I don't want her here, if that's what you mean," Emmet said, refusing to make eye contact with his sister, who was looking at the ground anyway.

"All right, then, what if Miss Harrington simply does her art nearby? That would be fine, yes?"

Emmet shrugged.

"Jolly good. Miss Harrington, you have your sketchbook with you?"

Lucy pointed to where she had been sitting on the other side of the wall and nodded.

"Well, then, it is decided." Mr. Williams slid one of the pool chairs along until it was against the wall, not two tortoise lengths away from me. "I simply want to ensure your dress does not become soiled," he said to Lucy with a wink. What a marvelous gesture, the wink. Her smile was resplendent.

And so, we remained in this formation for the subsequent suns, with Lucy alternating between drawing while listening, and simply listening.

"I'm not an idiot, you know," Emmet announced, responding to nothing in particular.

"No, certainly not," Mr. Williams said.

"I just don't see why I have to do this, and she doesn't."

"The reasons for that are more complicated, young Mr. Harrington, and will likely become clearer to you the more you learn and grow in this world."

"I wish I had to do this," Lucy said.

"You're such a square."

"Cut the gas, Emmet!"

"Now, now, my pupils. Shall we get back to work?"

But there was a slow trickle of activity beginning on the other side of the pool. Tables were being moved. More were arriving. A party. It was another party. Mother was busy directing the other women. When she noticed our merry band across the water, she paused, then made her way over.

"This is an unusual setup," Mother said matter-of-factly, as though a teacher, two children, and a tortoise together in an outdoor classroom were atypical.

Mr. Williams's energy contained something I had not yet felt from him before: nerves.

"We are having a wonderful day, Mrs. Harrington. Mr. Emmet has been doing excellent work."

She took a good look at me, but her eyes really lingered on Lucy. My presence was not the most noteworthy aspect of this scene for Mother.

"Is this where you've been hanging about when you come outside, young lady?"

Lucy nodded.

"She works on her drawings, and I thought she would be safer if I could keep an eye on her. Not to suggest there are dangers here, madam, not at all. I simply mean—"

"Of course, Mr. Williams. I understand perfectly well what you mean."

His energy changed as these words were uttered.

"This is a sound arrangement. No harm done. Emmet, you're working hard?"

"Yes, Mother."

"Good." She stared intently at Lucy. "I'm so pleased you're working on your art."

I thought I had seen the biggest smile Lucy's tiny frame could muster, but this one set a new record. I was elated by her elation. I was similarly delighted by the promise of this arrangement continuing, and in an officially sanctioned manner, to boot.

Then I noticed the decorations: red, white, and blue. The sky was to be lit up with explosions. It could be the very next moon, or the subsequent moon, or, more distressingly, multiple moons. I could not believe this was unfolding precisely as our educational endeavor was progressing so beautifully. As much as I wanted to remain in this precious pod of learning, every fiber of my being urged me to take leave. I had to begin my migration posthaste.

I stood up to my full height, and all three people looked over in surprise, presumably with understandable admiration for my stature. I set off in the direction of the sunset at a smart pace.

"Where are you going, Magic?"

The sound of her voice grabbed my heart.

"What do you mean, 'magic'? That's a table," Emmet said.

"Please don't go," she implored.

I could not look back due to both the emotion it would bring and the urgency of the situation at hand.

"I think you have to just let it leave," Mr. Williams said. Still not an it, but otherwise wise words.

The matter of not being able to reciprocate is one that has plagued me since I first linked fates with Takeo. To be unable to explicitly share my thoughts and feelings with people, to be incapable of audibly expressing sympathy or empathy or compassion, to not be understood—well, *frustration* is a wholly inadequate descriptor, but will suffice.

I would have said: "Please do not worry, my beloved Lucy. I shall return promptly once the sky has been returned to peace. I will miss you dearly. Keep studying as much as you can before the ghastly event." And: "I have most enjoyed being welcomed into the educational endeavor, Mr. Williams." As well as: "Emmet, I am proud of you for not complaining too much further about your sister's presence in the learning pod." Concluding with: "My impending sense of doom notwithstanding, I am confident that we will be reunited and able to learn together again in due course."

I abandoned these words, for even imagining them caused me consternation. I needed singular focus and propelled my legs forward as efficiently as possible. I did not have a reliable estimate of the duration for this journey as it had been hundreds of setting suns since I had last taken it, and I had never before begun at the pool. As a result, expediency was top priority. It was often better to be safe than sorry, and particularly the case given the gravity of the situation.

My route was contiguous to the cages, and I wished the birds and Monkey strength and courage. I moved parallel to Takeo's favorite pond, then past the forest sanctuary, and the vibrant memory of the joy I had experienced within its shelter urged me forward, even as my legs began to feel heavy from the lengthy journey. As darkness descended, I could neither rest nor pause for refreshment.

As the first crackles began, the outline of my destination came into view, near my special egg location, yet even more remote and distinct in one specific way: It contained rocks, a broad assortment around which I would surround myself. They seemed smaller, a reflection of my perpetual growth and their immobilized, inanimate state. I had first settled on this location because it was as far as I could get from the central source of the homegrown explosions and was somewhat sheltered from those that originated beyond these walls. In that moment, I realized I might have also chosen this precise area because the rocks were shaped like other tortoises.

I did not have time to ponder the significance of this fact because a loud boom overhead startled me, and I stumbled, knocking my chin on one of the rocks. It stung but I collected myself and continued onwards. As the fury of terrifying light and sound began filling the night sky, I tucked into myself and commenced the waiting process. I pictured those I had seen recently: the caged birds and Monkey of course, the rabbit, the squirrels, the sparrows, the robin. I had heard blue jays and cardinals, so they were around too. I hoped everyone was in safety and would emerge in reasonable shape, and that those who had fled would make their way back to our union.

Finally, from inside myself, I watched the blue misty sky dance of dawn, but did not emerge. There was no need yet; no lessons to observe, no delicious flower and fruit gift to enjoy, no delight to experience with Lucy.

I expected that there would be at least one or two suns before the educational activities resumed. Mr. Williams might even be elsewhere, or perhaps he had remained in this place but in a state of relaxation, something only humans seemed able to do during such explosive times.

So, I waited throughout the sun, moving little. I continued to think of the others and heard occasional birdsong, but not the usual choir. It would take some time for any semblance of normalcy to return. The next moon, there were scattered eruptions but at a greater distance, beyond the walls. I was able to properly relish the much-needed rejuvenating power of slumber.

I felt the rain arrive just as the sun began to appear. It was a welcome cooling respite, and I extended my neck to enjoy the raindrops' caress. As the sun ascended, a magnificent rainbow painted the blue canvas overhead. I must admit, the vivacity with which it illuminated the sky animated me. It was almost as if the sky sought to show people that its true sources of beauty are accompanied by the sound of silence. I stretched all four legs and cautiously retraversed the rocks, ready to embark on my journey back to the hearth.

I was barely out of the rocky quadrant when Lucy appeared from over a little hill, glowing with the same light as the multicolored sky.

"Magic!" she called, running towards me. I did not stop or retreat into myself, but rather surged forward with new zest in my steps.

"I'm so glad I found you," she said. She had mud on her knees, which may have resulted from a tumble, or perhaps from kneeling on the wet ground to peer into or under something. What was clear was that she had been looking for me. My heart sang.

"There was a party, which was okay, but I didn't really know anybody." She was walking beside me. She slowed her pace to match mine and regaled me with details of what I had missed.

"My dad came but he's gone again. I was telling him about you."

"They gave me a hot dog, but I only ate the bun with ketchup."

"I brought you this." She stepped in front of me, and unwrapped and then held out what I initially thought was a piece of orange. Yet its color was deeper and richer. It looked scrumptious.

"I hope you like mango. It's one of my favorites. I thought you might be hungry."

I stopped in order to properly partake. Oh my, this was a memorable experience. Its flavor surged.

"You eat cute!" she said giddily.

Once I had devoured the entire slice of heaven, I began to walk again, cognizant of the length of the journey ahead. Lucy stayed quietly beside me. We listened to the birds, more of whom were beginning to return and share their songs, and I found great pleasure in her company. We maintained a good pace all the way to the cages, where we both paused. The birds and Monkey were still out of sorts, which was not surprising given their proximity to the explosions from which they could neither retreat nor escape. Monkey was lying down facing the back wall and the birds were flitting about in a state of anxiousness. I could offer little comfort.

"I'm sorry, Monkey," Lucy said, sitting down on the ground. "I know you're scared."

Monkey turned around upon hearing Lucy's voice, and they locked eyes.

"I'm going to help you, little one," she said, her voice summoning a quiet yet assured determination I had not heard before.

One of the women from the house was in the vicinity, still cleaning up odds and ends from the festivities.

"Ven para la casa, mi lucecita," she called, nodding towards the residence.

Lucy sighed and stood up. "I will see you all soon, my beautiful friends."

The warmth lingered as she walked away. Monkey began to gently play with the ball.

I surveyed the pool area and noticed something new sketched on the wall of the learning pod. I opened my eyes wide and moved closer to get a better look. In soft green, there was a drawing of a brilliantly spherical individual with four strong legs and a graceful neck and head. Written above it, in beaming yellow, was "Magic."

Imperfect Unison

THIS WAS A spectacular time that I hoped would reach forward endlessly. Over the course of nearly fifty suns, I learned crucial insights about language and grammar along with a smorgasbord of social and geographic matters. Each of these dimensions was valuable in its own distinct way, and together this foundational knowledge made it possible for me to augment and refine my understanding of those around me and the world we shared in compelling ways. I gathered extensive information about Lucy that summer as well, which was especially meaningful. Delightful facts such as her favorite color (green) and songs ("Book of Love" by the Monotones, which is indeed catchy), and larger matters of significance, particularly the genuine and expansive nature of her compassion.

Mr. Williams began reading aloud later in the day specifically for Lucy, after Emmet had finished his lessons and moved on, plane in hand, to wreak havoc somewhere. We covered a range of contemporary and classic texts of greater and greater complexity. I believe that these readings provided the most influential and multifaceted learning of all, for they helped me better grasp the nuances of people's overt and hidden emotions, empathize with the struggles of even those who were very different from me, and see how the seemingly dissimilar may, in fact, be connected. My formal education was a very inclusive experience, and the safety of the community within which I learned was essential to my impressive intellectual growth. The power of belonging really cannot be overstated, for it both invites and reaffirms.

Moreover, not only was our learning collaborative, but it was also active and participatory. While the learning pod was our base, we would also extend out into different gardens at times, the textures and shapes of the plants an encouraging landscape that helped engage our bodies and spirits as well as our minds. Mr. Williams would ask Takeo to share elements of his extensive knowledge, and we enjoyed vivid lessons about specific plants, flowers, and trees, which were very illuminating. Lucy had many questions for Takeo, and he seemed to take great pride in both the fact that she would ask him and that he had meaningful answers to provide. Education really is a noble pursuit in many senses.

One afternoon, following a mesmerizing lesson about bees and their pollinating work (utterly marvelous), Emmet ran off towards the residence while Lucy walked even closer to me than usual.

"Mr. Williams, do you know where Magic is from?"

A question of utmost importance.

Yet Mr. Williams looked at Lucy quizzically. "Oh, you mean the tortoise?"

"Yes, of course. That's what I said: Magic."

"Right. Magic the tortoise!"

I turned my attention to Mr. Williams, and what was going on became clear. He was stalling. Lucy, ever sharp of mind, noticed as well.

"Do you know where Magic is from?"

Mr. Williams could delay no longer.

"Well, Miss Lucy, I am afraid I do not. I believe large tortoises such as your fine friend Magic here may be from South America, though it could be Africa."

Lucy crinkled her nose. "Those are two different continents."

Mr. Williams looked to be digging into the soil of his memories but found no roots.

"Was Magic born there or here?" she asked.

"Of that level of detail, I am most uncertain. Perhaps you could ask your uncle?"

"Maybe."

I did not feel at all confident that Ralph would possess such insight, nor that he would particularly care about my origins.

"Where is Monkey from?" Lucy asked.

"I am afraid I do not know that information either."

"I think Monkey is sad and lonely."

Mr. Williams looked towards the cages and nodded gently. "I do believe that is true." He turned back to Lucy and took a deep breath. "What would you like to read next, Miss Lucy?"

"*Alice's Adventures in Wonderland?*"

Was this the Alice Lucy had mentioned? What a splendid possibility!

"Mother read it to me before, but I would like to hear it again, and maybe I could try to read some pages myself?"

This book required great concentration due to the inclusion of older language from Mr. Williams's homeland, and the unusual and ambitious nature of so much of the action. Lucy asked many questions, and Mr. Williams would sometimes share the correct response, while on other occasions he responded to her queries with yet another query. I believe this was part of his teaching method: to not always provide the answer but rather to encourage Lucy to consider and reflect herself.

I listened intently and grappled with fact and fiction and

the occasionally tricky spaces in between. Once we were midway through the book, one day's reading began with an affirming discussion of Alice's assertion of her right to think. She had me convinced. It seemed a most basic right. What happened next, I could not have predicted. Alice encountered the Mock Turtle. I had never heard myself, or even someone remotely like me, represented before.

I had high hopes that this shelled individual would be a triumphant addition to Alice's life and her wondrous journey through Wonderland. Lucy, too, listened with the sharpest of focus as Mr. Williams read the Mock Turtle's story with his customary enthusiasm and articulateness.

Yet instead of feeling triumph, the Mock Turtle was sad. In fact, he no longer considered himself a real turtle. He had gone to school, albeit under the sea, which I would never do, but I understood this was a story, so accepted its embellishments and factual liberties due to the deeper insights it offered. In fact, the Mock Turtle had been taught by a tortoise. It turned out this was not actually a tortoise, but rather a turtle who "taught us" and therefore was called tortoise because of the similar sound. That was mildly disappointing but admittedly clever wordplay.

The Mock Turtle also spoke of an extra level of education available to some turtles but could not afford the additional lessons himself. I found this tragic. What sort of a shortsighted society would limit access to education? Would deny its members the opportunity to grow intellectually and gain the depth of knowledge, understanding, and skill that would allow them to better serve others?

I kept trying to keep up with the plot (lobsters were added into the mix, for example, which was challenging to imagine) while simultaneously deciphering what this text revealed about my kind. Then Mr. Williams handed Lucy the book.

"Try this song," he said. "There are some peculiar Victorian words, but I can certainly help with those."

She looked closely at the pages but said nothing. This continued for some time.

"Would you like to try reading it aloud?" Mr. Williams asked.

Lucy kept staring at the book. Then she spoke. "He is being asked to sing a song about soup made from him?"

Mr. Williams did not immediately reply but then said "May I?" as he reclaimed the book and read the page.

"Yes, well, I suppose that is the case."

I was disgusted. Aghast. Appalled at all the layers of indignity. Lucy's face was neutral, but I am completely certain that was performative.

"Ah, but look, there is a trial next," Mr. Williams said, and continued to read.

Although I did not know it then, I believe this was when I first realized there needed to be better stories about tortoises, told by tortoises.

Not long after, I became accepted at social gatherings around the pool, and this was a promising evolutionary step—for adults, I mean. I enjoyed watching people dance and listening to the music. Something particularly special also began to happen: Lucy would proactively introduce me.

"Ladies and gentlemen, may I present Magic," she would pronounce to various gasps and oohs and aahs and, regrettably, the occasional less pleasant sound effect or comment. Lucy would proceed, undeterred. "I ask that you do not poke Magic. Magic does not care for being poked and will disappear. Well, not totally disappear, but you know what I mean."

"That's a turtle?" someone would inevitably ask and be corrected.

"Why did you name it Magic?" one woman queried.

"Have you ever seen someone so magical?" Lucy replied.

When the sun began to spend less time overhead and the darkness arrived earlier, I felt the children's energy shifting, even before I heard open discussions about why. Emmet would be leaving for school and remaining there for long periods of time (by human standards). More significantly, Lucy would also be departing, but returning before darkness. I was not thrilled by this news. However, had she been in a situation like Emmet's, I would have been far more despondent.

Mr. Williams stayed later than usual one day to finish the latest Doctor Dolittle story and discuss its resolution with Lucy. Then he made the grim announcement.

"Miss Lucy, I am afraid that this is our last day together."

"What? Already?" She was visibly distraught.

"In mere days you will be off to school, where you will continue to experience new things."

"I will work hard."

"I know you will, I am most certain you will shine. My dear, you might even be a bit bored and find that some lessons are being repeated."

She looked down.

"Might I offer you some advice?"

Lucy nodded.

"Although I am by no means an expert on little girls, I know something of what it is like to not easily belong. As a result, I hope my counsel will be of use to you. Miss Lucy, even if you know every answer, do not offer them all. Choose only some responses to share, so that others may also answer, or, even, let there be silence."

"I don't understand. You mean don't answer when I know the answer?"

"Not every time. Do answer, yes, do answer, and make sure the teacher calls on you. But I have the utmost confidence that you will know significantly more than everyone else." He paused. "Sometimes people do not want girls to know as much as they do."

Lucy looked down again.

"Even some other girls might not want you to be as smart as you are."

Lucy was still for some time, then nodded. "I understand."

"Teaching you was a genuine pleasure, Miss Lucy Harrington. As a parting gift, I pursued something which I sincerely hope will be amiable to you."

Lucy's head tilted. So did mine.

"A former employer has monkeys at her rural residence. They live in a larger area with trees as a group. Each one came from elsewhere, and she speaks of trying to make amends for what others have done to them. Noble, indeed, and she really is quite a visionary. She is most willing to take over the care of Monkey. I took the liberty of discussing the matter with your uncle Ralph, on your behalf, not because I wish to speak for you, but rather to amplify your voice, if you will."

"Monkey could have monkey friends?"

"Yes, exactly, and Ralph was amenable. Are you pleased by this news?"

Her eyes glistened as they filled with tears. "I am delighted." She paused. "Thank you for everything, Mr. Williams." Tears slid down her cheeks.

I understood with all my heart. He had not only seen her hiding around that corner, he had really seen her.

In that moment, Mr. Williams betrayed something that would

be hard for someone with a less astute eye to perceive. I observed it, but it is even harder to describe. I felt it as a flurry in my heart.

He stood up and gathered his books and the globe he had brought out on his very first day and every lesson since, a perpetual physical reminder that while we are in this place, there is an entire world out there, for worse and for better. "Magic, you keep well," he said to me, tipping an imaginary hat. "In the words of the great Emily Dickinson, hope is the thing with feathers." With that, he walked away.

But Lucy called to him. "Mr. Williams!" He turned around. "Do you think birds are things?"

He looked puzzled by the question, then smiled. "No, well, I venture they are not, in fact, things."

Lucy nodded. "I agree."

I do not know where he went next or who else he taught. He did not return the following summer, or any subsequent summer. Yet his impact in this place was immeasurable, its melodies and out-of-tune chords alike; of that I am certain.

I accepted the transition of Lucy's schooling and understood the importance of her ongoing formal education. When Lucy went to school, I would engage in more regular communion with Takeo, who would kindly select treats for me here and there. I could see the effects of time and the physical demands of his job as he began to move more slowly, and both bend down and stand up with more difficulty. Yet he kept working, diligently tending to all the floral life with militant care.

My mind did feel unsatiated and hungry for more knowledge when Lucy was elsewhere, however. Thankfully, on school days, she would come running upon her return to look for me and then regale me with stories. She tended to share in a nonchronological and less ordered way, concentrating primarily on what she had studied that meant most to her, but I managed to follow along easily and learned many more new things through her retellings. She was a vivacious storyteller and could recount specifics from the lessons in immense detail. At times, I would imagine that I was in the classroom or library or museum with her. She was, understandably, very bothered when she learned that a dog had been sent way up into the sky. It was a prospect I found most perplexing not only because of my worry for the dog, but also because even after significant time spent pondering this "space race" about which adults spoke often, I still could not fathom why anyone would want to be anywhere but this extraordinary earth. I felt certain the dog did not wish to leave.

On the whole, I was delighted for Lucy's intellectual journey yet, admittedly, wished we really could be learning side by side, and felt some envy. I am not proud of that, though envy is preferable to feeling jealousy, with its sharper edges and consequences.

Time passed, and whenever the heat of summer returned, Lucy would spend her days here once again. I cherished our expanded time together with fervor. From time to time she would disappear for multiple suns in a row along with Mother and Emmet. She would share certain stories from these trips to the other side of the country and its cities, but mostly seemed pleased to be back with me among the flowers and bees. I began to worry less about Lucy leaving in a more permanent sense because she always returned.

One seemingly normal summer morning, as I patiently awaited Lucy's emergence from the residence by dozing in the shade, people from the house descended for party preparations. Beginning such preparation in the morning was unusual. Others then arrived to assist them, suggesting that this was an even more ambitious gathering than the usual social fare. The far end of the pool area was transformed into a stage adorned with groupings of black chairs on either side.

A different crew of people brought black boxes of various sizes and in unusual shapes. Some were oblong and easily carried. Others were nearly as large as the people themselves. As soon as the mysterious items were opened, I could not contain my excitement. Instruments! Real instruments! There was to be a musical performance!

Mother appeared with Lucy, and the two watched the setup process as attentively as I did. The musicians tenderly removed their instruments and began to polish, tune, and create short bursts of melodic wonder. Where precisely to position myself for this momentous occasion was a significant matter. The location needed to be carefully chosen for optimal listening, watching, and feeling. I was certain that music created in our very presence would move the earth, and I would be able to experience its cascading vibrations through the soil. I could already feel its arrival through the scattering of preliminary sounds.

I decided to make my way to Lucy. Musicians stopped their preparations and stared at me as I crossed in front of them. Lucy and Mother walked right up to the stage, and I stood proudly at their side.

"I am Louise Harrington, and this is my daughter, Lucy. The owner, Ralph Chilton, is my brother and her uncle. Might you be so kind as to help Lucy understand your instruments in greater detail?"

I could hardly believe my good fortune. I listened intently, relishing every detail. Flutes, violins, violas, oboes, trumpets, the triangle, and, oh, the harp! I was giddy and mesmerized simultaneously. Each instrument had both a distinct identity and cherished place within this beautiful collection.

"Are you a traveling symphony?" Lucy asked.

"You could say that," the oboist replied. "Do you know *Peter and the Wolf*?"

She nodded but said nothing.

"Lucy." Mother nudged her gently. "Be gracious."

"Yes, we saw *Peter and the Wolf* last year."

"That must have been marvelous," the oboist replied.

Lucy shook her head ever so slightly.

"Lucy!" That was Mother, of course.

"You didn't enjoy it?"

"I liked the music very much. I didn't like the story."

Mother smiled awkwardly but the oboist was unfazed.

"My daughter feels the same way. Tonight's performance is *Swan Lake*, and I hope you enjoy it. Tchaikovsky is one of my absolute favorites."

Mother and Lucy thanked the musicians and then walked off in the direction of the residence. I found myself standing all alone in front of the stage, the occasional pair of eyes still studying me. I knew I could not remain right front and center and made my way to the learning pod, a location most befitting of the grandeur of the event.

I was able to enjoy a short siesta, although my primary focus was observation of the remaining preparations. It was quite an ordeal. Spotlights were even brought in, suggesting that this performance could extend into the darkness. Large flower arrangements in pots were placed along the sides of the pools, an attractive addition to the area I hoped might remain. A fleet of largely indistinguishable men in dark suits walked through, speaking to no one. One literally, in the correct meaning of the word, stopped in his tracks when he noticed my presence. He studied me and I him, then he moved on.

Guests arrived in gowns and tuxedos and mingled as servers floated among them carrying trays of food and drink. I was delighted when the Harringtons arrived, including Father, and even more so when Lucy (and Emmet) were seated at a table not far from me by Mother. Lucy seemed taller in her evening attire with its voluminous skirt. She looked around, studying the scene, and smiled when she noticed me tucked against the wall. Father told Mother he was going to say hello to someone named Bobby, and then moved towards a group of men near the front.

The musicians had become an orchestra, an astonishing forty different people, each with a magnificent instrument. They began playing a quiet song, which seemed to signal to the guests that it was time to be seated. It was lovely but brief. Silence descended and remained until a sound so gentle yet simultaneously eruptive rose up and filled the air. It expanded as more instruments joined in, each one perfectly interwoven. Even now, I feel a flutter in my heart remembering the sensation of being wrapped in such a beautiful yet mournful tapestry.

Then, seemingly out of nowhere, male dancers appeared onstage and proceeded to move in perfect synchrony. Next there were women and paired movements. I enjoyed the dancing immensely but, at times, would close my eyes to fully immerse myself in the sheer power of the music. The next group of dancers summoned my attention, however, and I remained transfixed. They were dressed in white and adorned with feathers. I admired their long and lovely necks, and the precision with which they moved. They were breathtaking.

The subsequent scenes became more confusing and complicated. A man danced towards the bird women, but he was hunting them! Then there was a woman who was a bird or a bird who was a woman, and the story, as well as the music, made me feel taut. I began to shift in place, and this drew the attention of one of the dark-suited men who was standing nearby like a statue. Lucy and I locked eyes. Her face betrayed angst. The rest of her family continued to stare at the stage, even Emmet. The dance ended with the central bird and the man both lying still, in a heap. The audience leaped to its feet and applauded.

It was a strange experience, that is what I will say, an emotional storm. It was completely unbeknownst to me that circumstances were about to get even more peculiar.

Some suns later, machines and men were brought to this place and made quite a racket. I watched from afar as they worked in a grassy area with scattered trees on the other side of the residence. They dug a large hole, dumped gravel in it, then filled it with water. I did not immediately approach, but it seemed to be a promising addition to the place, a pond I could use for cooling off due to its sloping slides. Takeo would likely add some foliage at its edges and nearby to further beautify the area. I looked forward to seeing what he could create and would revisit the locale in due course.

When I did, I was not alone. There were two unmistakable white birds, their necks exceedingly long and lovely, one in the water, the other resting on the shore.

That fall, I spent more time near the swans, who did not fly away for some reason despite not being held in cages. They had a peacefulness about them I enjoyed and were perfectly comfortable with my brief forays into the shallowest edges of the pond to cool myself. They would float in the water, or groom themselves, or doze in the grass, transforming temporarily into white spheres. Lucy enjoyed the swans' presence and spent many a quiet evening in the area at my side.

The pool area remained relatively calm, although on occasion Mother would have other women over. They would dine and drink or just drink under the umbrellas or out in the full rays of the sun. I would maintain some distance, seeking not to interfere and, truthfully, still unsure whether I would be welcomed in close proximity the way I was when Lucy was around. The subjects of these conversations were not particularly enriching, but I resumed my informal learning nevertheless, as I had done prior to Mr. Williams's arrival.

I learned that Lucy's father would continue to conduct the majority of his business elsewhere and that they might return to him in due course. The latter was of concern, yet the manner in which this topic was discussed left me unconvinced. What I mean is that I observed Mother speaking in a way that did not suggest authenticity. While I had few details about what had caused Lucy to arrive with only Mother and Emmet, I sensed it was a source of secret tension and displeasure.

Then, for a number of suns (ten? Maybe more? I did not begin counting at the outset, unaware of the gravity of what was about to take place), there was very little pretending—everyone was afraid. Lucy and Emmet were both home, even though this was unequivocally the time for school. At first, I was delighted by Lucy's unexpected break, but she was not permitted beyond the immediate vicinity of the pool, and a heavy tension both hung and circulated in the air. Every person in this place was anxious and spoke either extremely quietly or far too loudly.

I heard only pieces of conversations, not atypical by any means but significantly more frustrating than usual given the obvious seriousness of the situation. I managed to be in the orbit of multiple hushed (and alarming) discussions between Mother and Ralph about whether the children were "safer" in this place or "out east" or somewhere different altogether. He had an outburst about "the commies already having stolen his money and now they're putting the entire world in danger." Father appeared and had a heated conversation with Mother, who sat stroking Lucy's hair.

"I don't know why you're acting like this, Louise!" he shouted. "This really could be it."

After he stormed off, Lucy joined Emmet, and Mother sat quietly together with them, his face pale and stoic in a way I had not seen before. He and Lucy even held hands.

"If the world is ending, I want to be here," Lucy said tearfully.

"Oh, sweetheart. The world isn't ending," Mother said, although her face betrayed something different.

I moved closer and stood beside Lucy. I think it calmed both of us. The next day I saw her hugging Takeo when he came near the pool. Then he was nowhere to be seen.

The fear was contagious, and no person was immune. I struggled to offer sagacity and peacefulness for Lucy in particular, while my mind desperately grasped at what bits of information I could glean and process. I was trying to conceptualize what it would mean if the world ended. If there were no world. I pictured Mr. Williams's globe with many different continents, home to countless species, nations, and families. The oceans, too, they were home to so many aquatic animals. Did Ralph and Mother and Father really mean that everything and everyone could be gone? I could not comprehend what humans could do that would cause damage of that scale and severity, yet somehow, I knew it was possible. I knew this both intellectually and emotionally. Time stretched out and I ached with worry.

Then suddenly, everything shifted, and people became relaxed again. I was elated yet positively exhausted and slept right through multiple suns in a row. For a long time afterwards, long even by my standards, I thought that was the most afraid people could be.

Red, Gold, and Green

FOLLOWING THAT TERRIFYING period, the rhythms returned to normal. Lucy was again permitted to extend out into this place late in the day once home from school, although the darkness was arriving earlier along with cooler weather, and this limited our time for interaction and contemplative reflection.

Then, without warning, she simply stopped emerging. An insufferable period passed without Lucy's presence. I needed to know what was going on and desperately wanted to find Lucy. In this anxious state, I seriously considered doing something I had done only once prior: approaching the residence directly.

The first time I had done so was during my initial exploration and documentation period. I had followed the hard path that extended beyond the pool and was wrapped on both sides by palm trees. I passed behind the vehicle storage buildings, then arrived at the mouth of another outdoor seating area at the back of the main residence with a central table and small fountain. A man nearby noticed me. This was even before the arrival of Takeo and Ralph, and the man was not someone I had seen before. For safety,

I immediately retreated into that much smaller version of myself. The man proceeded to use a broom to push me right off the path and away from the residence! The sensation brought me both physical and mental discomfort, and I felt most unwelcome.

Needless to say, the memory of this unfortunate incident, however distant it was, did not fill me with confidence about how I would be received at the residence, my new status as cherished companion to Miss Lucy notwithstanding. Since I had been unable to sufficiently document the terrain directly adjacent to the residence, I also lacked certainty in my ability to successfully traverse its obstacles. As a result, I opted to simply place myself nearby, hoping that Lucy would soon return. I settled into an area with ample ground foliage for cover but with an unobstructed view of the back of the residence. Fifteen suns later, I had yet to see or hear my beloved Lucy. There were no Harringtons around at all, in fact.

I felt a renewed sense of cautious hope when red, green, and gold decorations were placed around the pool, though I have no logical explanation for why I do not care for Christmas songs despite being both a musical connoisseur and a fan of the festive season. (Wham! and, of course, the illustrious Ms. Mariah Carey provide amiable exceptions to the seasonal canon, but this was well, well before their creation and ascendancy.) Surely the pool area would be a site for social gatherings and the resulting good cheer. Lucy would return. Lucy had to return.

Yet it was Ralph and other non-Harrington adults who appeared periodically, not Lucy. I became forlorn, and even Takeo's most generous offerings did not lift my spirits. I did not care for this drought one bit or how little I knew about what was happening.

Mercifully, it finally came to an end. The Harringtons, including Father, arrived one evening in fancy garb. Lucy was even taller, and there was something different about her I could not decipher.

She quickly made her breakaway from the party, in the direction of the forest sanctuary. She had not seen me in my hideout.

I became animated when I spotted her meandering back towards the pool area before the arrival of darkness. I stepped out from beside the building's wall and protective blanket of flora so I would be impossible to miss.

"Magic!" she called, and sped up her pace. Strangely, she did not begin regaling me with stories or provide any information of value about what she had been doing or where she had been. She studied the ground, clearly deciding whether or not to sit down and face the wrath of Mother for soiling her festive frock, and opted not to. Instead, she stood very close to me and simply looked around, taking in the beauty of the trees, bushes, plants, and flowers. She sighed.

"I've missed you all," she said.

Next, something extraordinary happened. She studied me closely. "I've really missed you, Magic. How have you been?" And with those words, she touched me.

It was not a poke—quite the opposite in fact. It was a soft stroke of my neck. I held her gaze as I processed the feeling. This was an unusual physical sensation, one I had never experienced before. But even more than that, I was moved by the gentleness of the gesture. I believe her prior refusal to touch me was out of respect. Her adamant directions to adult guests at parties about them refraining from poking me certainly indicated an awareness of how I felt about human contact. Prior to that moment, I had been touched by human hands during the coerced exile from my homeland, during those dreadful early days of incessant examination, when I was again moved to this place, and whenever people felt like ogling or tearing around with the younger, smaller, and lighter version of me. Takeo had also touched me and done so respectfully, but for functional reasons. Being moved into the wheelbarrow was a happy memory, but an exception among the general pattern of hand-to-tortoise contact. Yet, in that moment, Lucy demonstrated that human touch could mean something else: Affection. Kindness with no ulterior motive.

I felt a warmth waving through my body and wanted it to continue indefinitely. The feeling was calming and reassuring. All my worry evaporated as I embraced our harmony.

"I'm so glad to see you," she said, removing her hand. Something, or rather someone, had solicited her attention on the far side of the pool. As she walked away, she turned back. "Merry Christmas Eve, my angel."

Outdoor Christmas Day antics did not begin until well into the sun's ascendancy, but I had been bold and placed myself back in the learning pod in anticipation of poolside socializing of some sort and, most significantly, Lucy's return. Knowing she would be present gave me a revived sense of confidence about my ability to be positioned right in the heart of the human action, particularly in combination with the heightened joy and frivolity that accompanied the occasion.

I was therefore pleased when a tornado of children surged down the path, despite not recognizing some of them. Lucy spotted me right away and made a beeline for my location. She had on a red-and-green sweater (or jumper, as Mr. Williams would call it) with animals on the front. Without even a word of greeting, she stood firmly in front of me, seemingly anticipating what would come next. A pair of unknown boys were loudly running about and diverted their course when they noticed me.

A girl around Lucy's size arrived first and stared at me.

"Gosh," she said. "I've never seen anything like that."

"This is Magic," Lucy said to her, keeping her eyes on the boys as they approached.

"What you got there, ankle biter?" the taller one said. "What a weird creature."

"Please go away. You are not to touch," Lucy said. I took note of the fact that she had opted not to introduce me to them.

"What are you going to do to stop me?" the other boy said. This degree of hostility was not something I had expected during such a celebratory time, and I found it rather unsettling. I could sense Lucy's energy and that she was feeling the same way.

"You guys, don't. It's Christmas," the girl said.

Adults appeared and the children other than Lucy dispersed as their parents began sitting down around the pool. Mother, Father, and Ralph were among them, but Father settled at a separate table with an older white-haired man. Lucy remained in my vicinity. The learning table had been removed, but there were lounge chairs in the shade designed for the length of most human bodies. She sat down in one of them, and I noticed just how much longer her legs had become.

As she opened a book, I felt a minuscule sensation on my back, and Lucy looked over at me. I had to turn my neck awkwardly to see what had happened and could catch only a glimpse. Someone had stealthily placed a red bow on me. I was not sure how to feel about it at first or what it meant. But Lucy smiled and the other girl appeared and admired me (it turned out she had placed the bow), then some adults joined in, along with Emmet, who was significantly taller as well. As a result, I accepted the bow and its placement on my person as a reflection of the joy of the occasion.

"Magic does not normally wear clothes but is certainly a gift," Lucy said. Emmet added a second bow, which I thought might be excessive but tolerated in the spirit of the season and a well-intentioned gesture from a boy who was not always well-intentioned.

The joviality I had expected became the norm as light conversation and laughter continued. The only unfortunate dimension was that it did not veer into the terrain of my most sought-after topic—Lucy's recent whereabouts and her intended location for the post-Christmas period. As the sun began to descend, the human crowd thinned out.

Mother wandered over and smiled at me. "Well, don't you look festive," she said. "Lucy, we should go in. It's almost time for dinner."

"Just a few more minutes?"

Mother kissed Lucy on the top of her head. "That's fine, sweetheart. I know you've missed this place. Enjoy your time with Magic."

The pool area became quiet and peaceful. Emmet and the other boys were running around but did so some distance away and were not making too much noise. Lucy was enthralled with her book, and I with her presence. It was blissful and exactly what I wanted for Christmas, though I did wish she would read aloud so I could share in the captivating literary journey.

Lucy then rose and made her way to the nearest garden. I walked towards her, intrigued by what she was up to. She moved here and there, and assembled an appealing cross section of flowers, which she subsequently presented to me at the garden's edge.

"Merry Christmas, my dear friend Magic."

I partook in the bouquet with pleasure, enjoying the combination of distinct flavors as I dined. Lucy returned to her chair, and I tidied up some of the delicate greenery that had tumbled during my enthusiastic mastication. Lucy once again began reading intently, mesmerized by the contents of the pages. I was impressed by her expanding reading abilities, albeit not surprised in the least, given her intellectual prowess heightened further by her drive and persistence.

I was thinking of the pushmi-pullyu from Doctor Dolittle

when, out of nowhere, we were ambushed. The two boys from the initial unpleasant exchange had returned. No one else was around. The shorter one knocked the bows right off my back. The other boy tossed Lucy's book onto the ground, then started rapidly touching under her arms and down her sides, placing his hands all over the animals on her sweater.

"I don't like that," she said, trying to escape his grasp.

He kept touching her.

"Donald, don't. It's not funny."

He pinned her down.

"Stop!"

He covered her mouth with his free hand. "You are such a know-it-all." She was trying desperately to kick at him and scream, but only muffled sounds were emerging, and he overpowered her with ease.

I was enraged. I began to move in their direction to aid Lucy somehow, furious at the inadequacy of even my fastest pace.

"You're going to hurt her," the shorter boy said, nudging the book with his foot.

"I'm just tickling her. She's a crybaby."

A voice yelled from near the residence. "Boys, it's time to eat!"

Donald stared down at Lucy.

"We should go," the younger one said, beginning to walk away.

Donald kept staring at Lucy as he released her. Then he looked right at me. He picked up the book and threw it at my head before I could react. I felt the blow just below my eye as the book ricocheted to the ground. All I could do was hiss.

"Oops," he said as he walked away. "Merry Christmas."

Lucy did not move a muscle until the boys disappeared. She wiped the tears from her face and straightened out her sweater.

"Are you okay?" she asked, studying me. She began stroking my neck again. So many emotions were swirling around that I could not properly think. I watched her walk all the way back to the residence.

The lights circled the pool and bounced off the water, which swayed ever so slightly in the breeze. An owl hooted in the distance. The hard ground was uncomfortable, but rather than seeking softer terrain, I pulled my legs inside. The bows were splayed out on the concrete. I remained in place in some pitiful attempt to guard the book, the tale that had so captivated Lucy, a pig and a spider adorning its cover.

Lucy did not reemerge the next day. I moved into my quiet lookout and waited for twenty suns and twenty moons. Then twenty more. As the days got longer and sunnier, Takeo paused to pull a flower from a nearby garden and offered it to me before rushing off. I partook, but it brought me no pleasure.

Depths

I WAS IN the dark about Lucy and her whereabouts, and a heavy opaqueness enveloped my very being. When the overwhelming urge to retreat to the dark and cool area near the back wall arrived, the importance of the task at hand became my focus and beacon. That provided temporary mental respite while I journeyed. However, once my eggs were placed, the dark cloud redescended and I kept to myself. The free birds sang, but I could not hear them.

I remained in this forlorn state for quite some time. On occasion I wandered listlessly, yet often I remained sedentary. I moved around enough to suspect and then confirm another giant void. Takeo was nowhere to be seen. Takeo was gone.

In retrospect, I believe I slid into a pit of despair because I had experienced such authentic care and been shown a different side of humans. The birds, the squirrels, the rabbits, every one of them was kind to me. But people have been more complicated. Takeo and I had become true friends. I loved Lucy and she loved me. We had learned so much together. These were connections without any pretention or transaction that were rooted in kindness. I had felt deeply, so the pain was immense. The more you care, the more losses hurt.

Only Ralph was around infrequently and he looked to be unwell. Gone were the days (and nights) of his debaucheries and family gatherings alike. On occasion a single guest or a small number of visitors would sit with him near the pool, but never enter it. One woman was with him often, but she was different from his usual companions, who were always the epitome of high-maintenance glamour. This one seemed to be focused entirely on his health: a nurse, not a date or dalliance.

For reasons I could not understand, as time stretched forward and Ralph's body continued to deteriorate, some guests brought him animals, seemingly as gifts. A donkey was dropped off and a fence erected to contain them in a small grassy quadrant, mercifully with some trees for shade at least. Then an alpaca. A cat who was allowed to roam right away. More birds in cages. One guest delivered a large red bird with rainbow wings. Because of my anger at this unfairness without end, along with my overall state of despondency, I could not bring myself to greet any of these new residents, let alone to properly welcome them and lend my support. Other than laying my eggs each year, I kept myself largely still and isolated.

Finally (how much later I cannot say for certain, maybe a thousand suns), following a sprinkling of rain, the sky became a portrait, as though a painter of immense talent had delicately slid watercolors across it. I was instantly reminded of Lucy and experienced the pain of her absence anew. Yet I was also able to summon what she had shared with me, and the joy I had felt as a result. I thought of Takeo and the first vibrant pink flower he had given to me, and all his subsequent generosity. I was able to use these feelings to enliven my body and propel my steps. I ultimately realized I needed to begin my own journey again. I began the voyage to see the new resident with rainbow wings.

The parrot was being kept in Monkey's former cell. I approached and admired the vibrancy of their feathers. The bird was staring right back. In fact, they seemed to be studying me. I rested on my stomach and tried to appreciate the colors and songs of the area, as well as firmly establish my unwavering commitment to all of these birds. I dozed off in the heat of the day.

When I awakened, I stood up to stretch my legs and neck. The parrot tilted their head. Well, I could not believe what happened next. The bird made such an unusual and startling noise. It was a bold squawk. I had never heard anything like it. Then the unquestionably stunning bird emitted a discernible sound that was unmistakable. The bird spoke human! What transpired next is rather amusing in retrospect: I thought the bird was introducing herself as Ola. Repeatedly.

I still chuckle about that now and learned the error of my ways not long after. In that moment, I found it stupendous, and while I was certainly displeased by the bird's placement in a cage, I marveled at the impressiveness of her linguistic abilities. I felt some envy, I must admit, but was firmly committed to thinking positive thoughts. I was earnestly attempting to will my body and spirit back to their former glory, or perhaps instead usher in a newfound sense of stubborn contentment combined with heightened caution about not caring too much about people due to their tendency to disappear. That such a remarkable creature would be kept behind bars by humans furthered my dissatisfaction with the overall state of affairs, yet unfortunately, I was not surprised. Nevertheless, I remained steadfast in my refusal to fall back into melancholy.

While I was enthusiastic about meeting the donkey and the alpaca and providing them with an overdue welcome, their fenced enclosure was some distance away on the far side of the residence. My failure to generously greet the new residents upon arrival and serve as a hospitable host to help them transition to this place was now a fait accompli. I regretted my actions, and specifically my inaction, but opted not to dwell on that which could not be altered. I could be derelict in these duties for some suns longer without consequence and then begin the process of making up for my delinquency through a proper welcoming.

I focused on demonstrating my solidarity with Ola, someone I wanted to both support and impress. As the sun extended and then descended, I carefully studied all the caged birds. Along with the new arrivals, there were, regrettably, some departures who I felt certain had not been returned to their homelands.

The next sun, Ola started the day by adding what I interpreted to be her last name. Ola Chica seemed to be as chuffed about me as I was with her, despite my inability to verbally reciprocate. I would have introduced myself as Magic but added that Daisuke was also perfectly acceptable, sentimental as I was. Undeterred by my silence, Ola Chica continued to share her name as she hopped around her cage, which had been adorned with a wooden stand. It was a sort of miniature tree, not a palm tree but rather one resembling the multibranch varieties that reside in the forested areas. Perched atop this structure was where she spent most of her time.

The sun had not even begun to reach its peak when what I spotted in the distance made my heart leap. Not what, but rather who. Takeo was walking towards me! Takeo, who seemed to have done the impossible and, instead of aging, had grown younger. As he arrived in front of me, I realized this was, of course, not actually Takeo.

"Could this really be the famous Daisuke in the flesh?" the man said to me.

I was astonished. Not only was this man aware of me, but he also knew my name. Takeo had spoken of me!

"Good to meet you, fella."

"Ola!" the parrot said.

"Yes, hello to you too."

"'Hola, preciosa' is better, I think." This was a woman's voice, behind me. "Maybe for both of them." She laughed a perfect joyful song. It was the woman who had been tending to Ralph.

"Maybe for the parrot, but this here's Daisuke." He nodded in my direction.

"I heard that it had been named Magic. Or at least I had heard of a Magic, but it seemed too strange, even for this place. I thought that it was gone or had . . ." She trailed off. I knew what she would have said but did not dwell on it. My emotions were bounding like a rabbit. Lucy's name for me lived on too, a glowing legacy commemorating her spirit and our connection.

"And what is your name?"

"Michio Yamada. If it's easier, you can call me Mitch."

"I think I can manage Michio, compañero. My name is Clara."

"It's a pleasure to meet you, ma'am. You're Mr. Chilton's nurse, is that right?"

"Did this give me away?" She laughed again, gesturing at her outfit. I could listen to her laugh all day. Then her expression became more serious, and she said, "I am working as his nurse, yes, that's right."

She opened a small container and placed some nuts and seeds as well as a grape into a tray suspended from one of the bars in Ola's cage. Clara put the rest in similar trays attached to the other cages. These feeding contraptions were an upgrade from when I had last been in the area.

"Michio, I am very sorry for your loss and would like to express my sincere condolences. Your dad had such skill. I marvel at his artistry." She looked around. "But more than that, he showed everyone kindness."

"Thank you very much. He was my grandfather. I hope I can

honor his memory. He left some very big boots to fill. And gardens to manage!" Michio's face shifted into a warm smile. He reminded me a lot of Takeo, maybe what Takeo would have looked like when he was a young man.

"He was very good to my nephew and found him work. That meant a lot to my whole family, and it would not be an exaggeration to say that the insurance from the Gardeners' Federation saved my nephew's life."

"Oh, I didn't know that, but am not surprised. He certainly understood what it's like trying to make your way in this country, especially when it's most difficult. After being forced to live in the desert at Manzanar, caring for flowers brought him peace. He quietly showed how to be kinder."

"The inescapable network of mutuality, as Dr. King would say." She paused. "Rest in power."

Michio nodded. "I still can't believe he's gone."

Silence hung in the air.

"Ola Chica!" interrupted the silence. The bird was staring at Clara and rocking back and forth, one foot then the other.

"Hola, preciosa," Clara admired the bird right back.

"Hola, preciosa." Michio repeated the words with little trouble.

"That's very good. *Preciosa* is 'precious' and, well, you know *hola*, I expect."

"Yes, ma'am."

"How do you say *hello* in Japanese?"

"At this time of day, *kon'nichiwa*."

"Kon'nichiwa," she said, and it was then that I understood. Ola was not a name; it was *hello*. Rather than feeling foolish, I focused on the fact that the parrot had taught me my first Spanish word.

"Hola, chica," she said.

Clara laughed. "Ay, eres encantadora. This is a charming bird. I hope you enjoy your meal, preciosa."

"If it would be easier for you, I'm happy to feed the birds," Michio offered.

"That is very kind of you, but I don't mind at all. In fact, I appreciate the opportunity to get away from the house and . . . everything there. I like coming out here and being with the birds. And you already have a lot of work to do." She gestured to this place in all its glory and laughed.

In this moment, my heart sang a little.

Clara. Michio. Preciosa.

Wonders Never Cease

MY MIND WAS reinvigorated and I processed everything I had learned throughout the peak sun, albeit from a cooler spot in the shade nearby with my legs in the soil. Preciosa was energized too and hopped from leg to leg on the makeshift tree after partaking in brunch.

Clara was mighty, yet filled with serenity too. I imagine it took a mountain of patience to tend to Ralph, especially in his current state. I had observed him being morose with people who worked here, although he still managed to put more of his classic charm on display for his occasional guests. Ralph was older, but more than that, his body was failing him. Takeo had never become impolite, even when the lines on his face deepened and his hair transitioned from black with strands of silver to almost completely white. He had aged with grace and gratitude, something I realized I wanted to do.

I had not thought about aging at all before, having no idea of how long tortoises generally spent on Earth to consider or compare. In fact, I could not even harbor a guess. I initially thought it possible that I could already be considered a senior (my naivety was almost endearing). I had been here for jazz and big band, but this knowledge did not help in any precise way because an unknown but undoubtedly large number of suns had passed before people brought their music into this place.

Observing both Takeo and Ralph suggested that human bodies slowed down. I hypothesized that this might not be a characteristic of tortoise aging, however. I knew the body or at least parts of it would become stiff and sore, and that sickness was more likely. In contrast, the mind would be so full as to become a treasure chest, overflowing with the gems from a lifetime of learning. I had amassed significant knowledge yet still had much to learn. As a result, I concluded that I was probably not old. I determined that, on balance, aging was a gift, one I would cherish when it arrived.

I was glad to know Takeo had a family and hoped I might be able to learn more about these details through conversations between Michio and Clara. Their families seemed to have had interwoven threads within and beyond these walls. Posthumous knowledge about Takeo was better than continuing to be ignorant about my first human friend.

"Have a nice day," Preciosa announced, to my complete astonishment. She was bilingual!

A group of three brown speckled free birds—towhees, I believe—flitted about the cages before landing on top of them. The trapped birds danced a bit but then stopped and peered up, studying their wild, soaring relatives. It was lovely in a way, this cross-barrier connection, but also brought a wave of sorrow that crashed into me and knocked me off-balance. How people decided what to do and not do with animals, even those who were very similar, was a mystery.

I allowed the feeling to remain but not drown me. Life without sadness was simply impossible. Pretending to be perfectly happy seemed neither plausible nor sustainable. I would feel sad because of losses. Daring to be connected means there will be disappointments, unrequited affections, and ruptures. Because I was highly attuned to those around me, their pain and longing would be a boulder pressing down on my spirit. I would need to learn to carry additional weight, for short and long journeys alike. I decided to feel the hurt of others not on top of me but rather behind me, propelling me forward.

I spent longer near the cages than originally planned since Preciosa was so thoroughly interested in me and because Clara would come by every morning. Preciosa knew other words, specifically "Nice try" and "Buenos días." Even though she possessed this extraordinary ability to communicate in the languages of another, what she said did not really illuminate her identity or personality. It exposed more about the people she had been with, those who had held her in the past, maybe even taken her from her homeland.

Preciosa's behavior provided greater insights into who she really was. She studied me and seemed intrigued by my movements in particular. Despite my size and shape being unbirdlike, she was fully aware that I was someone. I could not help but wonder if she had observed others like me before and what that might mean about where she had been, and where other tortoises were.

Clara often seemed to be in a hurry and would efficiently place the birds' brunch, share a few words with them in Spanish, and be on her way. When I was nearby but not directly adjacent to the cages, I do not think she saw me. On cooler days when I could handle the full pressure of the sun's rays and therefore positioned myself right close to Preciosa, Clara would greet me as Magic. This filled me with delight.

On one particularly memorable morning, she lingered for longer and began singing about flowers as an expression of love.

"Dos gardenias para ti. Con ellas quiero decir te quiero, te adoro, mi vida."

I watched this woman create such a beautiful melody, as if drawing from deep inside herself, and felt the vibrations through the earth. She looked through the bars and cages somehow not at the birds but rather with them. The birds stared back with wonder. She selected a grape from her offerings, which she presented to me. I graciously accepted and savored the flavor in concert with the sensory experience of her song.

Although Michio would pass by often enough on his way to or from one of the gardens, their schedules did not align. This was disappointing both for my own sake, since I had hoped their conversations would reveal more about Takeo, and because Michio and Clara seemed to have a warm, genuine connection. Through diligence and his own version of persistence, Michio was keeping this place beautiful. Takeo would have been proud, indeed. I continued to keep an eye on as much of the terrain as possible without abandoning Preciosa and friends. Clara would push Ralph around the gardens in a wheelchair. Then there was no sign of Ralph whatsoever.

When one bright sun was only beginning to appear, Clara arrived at the cages not in the usual white uniform, but rather in a flowing dress. At this early hour, Michio was nearby.

"Good morning, Clara. You look lovely."

"Thank you, Michio. Have you heard the news?"

"I don't think so."

"Ralph died last night. It was peaceful."

"Oh my."

Michio said nothing as Clara placed the food for the birds and watched them eat.

"Some family members are on their way."

Michio simply nodded. I believe we were all trying to process what Ralph's death might mean for this place and everyone in it.

"I think you will be okay, querido. I cannot imagine the family is going to give up somewhere like this."

"I hope that's true. Thank you. What will this mean for you?" Michio asked.

Clara smiled. "I am not certain yet. I may go back home."

"Oh, wow."

"I still have some family there. I don't know what that would be like exactly, but I might see how it goes. I believe I could be of help to more people back home."

"Would you keep working as a nurse?"

Clara smiled, but it was a different expression than simple joy. "I am actually a doctor. I think I would like to be a doctor once again."

She reached forward, and I could not believe what I witnessed next. One by one, she opened the cages. At first, the birds were not sure what to do and they did not make any movements. Then Clara stepped back. A bird flew right out through the opening, followed by another. And another. A couple of them settled on top of the cages and seemed to be getting their bearings. Others went directly to the nearby trees and perched on delicate branches. They began to sing their daily recognition songs, but these were more elaborate versions with additional notes and greater energy.

"I hope they will make it," Clara said.

Michio stood in silence, watching this all transpire. His face shifted into a gentle smile. "I hope so too."

Clara turned her attention to the one remaining bird, the largest and loudest of them all. Clara opened the gate to what had been Monkey's cell, then Preciosa's. Preciosa studied the opening but did not move.

"¡Hola, chica!" she said instead.

"Sí, sí. Hola, mi amor. You are free," Clara replied, gesturing to, well, everywhere. Preciosa flapped her wings in a manner more awkward than graceful and landed on top of the cage.

"You are free," Clara repeated.

Preciosa tilted her head, studying everything and everyone. Then she flew at Clara, who put up her hands to protect her face. But Preciosa slowed and landed gently on Clara's arm.

Clara started laughing, as did Michio. Clara lifted her arm, trying to toss Preciosa into the air, but the bird refused to let go. "Ay, ay, amor." Clara turned her arm to study the bird, and they looked right into each other's eyes. Then Preciosa hopped off Clara's arm and onto her shoulder. Clara stood in silence, seemingly stunned.

"Maybe there is magic here," Michio said.

Clara smiled and shook her head. "All right, well, Michio, please take care of yourself and your family. And"—she gestured around once again—"of this beautiful and mysterious place."

"I wish you the best," he said and bowed slightly. "Take care of as many people as possible."

"I will, and, well—" She tilted her head towards Preciosa, who looked as happy as a tortoise in shade. And with that, they were gone. Our precious time together had reached its end. I hope their journey together was just beginning and that it would be full of vibrancy in every language.

The heat made me sleepy, yet I was far too fired up to sleep. I was sad about Ralph. The end of a life is significant, any life. I considered how much time I had been indirectly alongside the man, remembering early moments, happy times, angry outbursts, strange acquisitions, all of it. I knew so little about him. Yet he was clearly a person of consequence in the larger world, as well as here. This was his place. His loss would have consequences.

During the golden hour, I spotted activity around the residence, but only outlines given the distance, no details. The next morning, a few people began to gather around the pool. My heart sped up. First, I recognized Mother. She was older, but not old, and still elegant. She hugged a young man who looked to be around Michio's age. After the embrace, I saw his face. It was Emmet! Emmet was tall now. Emmet was an adult! He, Mother, and another man I did not recognize began a conversation about some papers at one of the tables under an umbrella.

Then a young woman with long hair arrived. Mother and Emmet hugged her. My stomach was doing somersaults, and I stood to get a better look. I began marching in their direction. She shook hands with the other man and then stepped back. She turned to face the majesty of this place. I reached my fastest pace, heading directly for her.

"This cannot be possible," she said. Her eyes became glossy. She dropped onto her knees and wrapped her arms around my neck. It was weird, but wonderful.

"I can't believe it," she said. Tears slid down her cheeks. "Magic, you are still here. You are alive."

In fact, it was the most alive I have ever felt.

Duty of Care

I PARKED MYSELF right in the heart of the action and had no plans to leave. The man with the papers looked shocked as I stood smartly beside Lucy, then completely stunned when she stroked my neck. How I had missed her. The feeling pulled my body in all directions.

After discussions about how many people were employed and what they did, as well as their pay schedule, the man moved on. Lucy, Mother, Emmet, and a couple of other people ate around the pool and discussed a mix of inconsequential things and their memories of Ralph. There was a somber mood. Mother was reduced to tears a couple of times. Lucy's eyes filled to overflowing once. I was not able to glean much of value about what was to happen next, but I did induce that Lucy had begun college "out east" and, in completely unsurprising news, was earning top grades despite being a year younger than everyone else. Mother seemed pleased with this fact and, dare I say, proud.

They all returned to the residence, Lucy giving my neck one more gentle rub before making her way. The subsequent sun, she came out alone as the temperature was just beginning to cool.

Although my mind and spirit were practically levitating, I had held my body in place so she would see me immediately, and my plan worked brilliantly.

"I really can't believe you're still here," she said, smiling and shaking her head. She walked on, past me, seemingly intent on further exploring the state of this place. I desperately wanted to accompany her and for us to explore every single inch at tortoise pace, eating mangoes. Really, I wanted her to return for good, to spend every day reading and listening to the birds (wild birds only! Oh, how I longed for her to know that the caged birds had been granted freedom!).

I knew this was not possible. She was a young woman now, a scholar. She was spreading her own wings and soaring. I shifted my thinking to the possibility that this return might be the beginning of more visits at least.

The next sun, a small gathering of people of various ages in black walked through the gardens, the adults pointing things out for the youngest people, who were remarkably well-mannered. Lucy guided the children around to various locales, and then in my direction.

"When I lived here, this was my most favorite friend. May I present the illustrious Magic."

"Whooooa!" the boy said when he got closer. "It's like a dinosaur."

"Did you choose the name Magic?" the little girl asked. She reminded me a bit of a young Lucy. She possessed a similarly gentle yet animated energy and was not even a neck taller than me.

"I did, in fact. I think I was around your age."

"It's a perfect name. Hello, Magic. It's a pleasure to make your acquaintance."

My heart, well, it did a little jig.

"Lucy, are there still swans?" one of the gray-haired adults called.

They all walked off, presumably to see the swans, who were still somehow among us, despite not being in cages.

The next day was very quiet until the golden hour, when Emmet arrived with a group of other young men. They drank and swam and were altogether quite rowdy. I was tempted to vacate the area, but the prospect of Lucy returning held me like a magnet. They finally retreated to the residence when the light of the moon beamed down, and then I was able to properly enjoy slumber.

A similar pattern occurred the subsequent day; however, the golden hour brought not only young men, but young women as well. Music was added into the mix. Couples kissed in the shadows. As darkness descended, I kept a close eye on Lucy as she moved among the guests, never talking with anyone for too long. I admired her excellent dancing, then she walked away from the bluster of the festivities and seated herself on the edge of the pool near our cherished learning pod, her feet dangling in the water. I joined her and another young woman who had sat down.

"Oh my god!" the woman uttered as I approached. Lucy turned to see what had startled her friend and laughed. Not what, of course, but rather who.

"Jessica, this is my beloved Magic." I stopped beside Lucy. Jessica studied my beautiful shape. "I spent a lot of time with Magic the years I stayed here." Lucy stroked my neck.

"Only you would befriend a giant turtle!"

"Tortoise, technically. I don't know, I think Magic charmed a lot of people. She was always more polite than some of Uncle Ralph's guests, that's for sure. We had the best of times, didn't we, Magic?"

Jessica laughed, but it was true. Every word.

"Rest in peace, Mr. Ralph," Jessica said.

One of the boys jumped loudly into the pool and then another followed. A scattering of splashes reached all the way to us.

"He had so many animals. He collected them like ornaments. Even when I was little, it bothered me. My teacher at least found a home for a monkey who had been kept here. I hope that was better than the solitude of a cage. I still think about that sweet little animal."

As do I.

"Did Ralph really get a zebra?"

"Sort of. A zebra crossed with a donkey, apparently."

What?! What on earth was this information?

"That was one of the animals he got after I left. It's been so long since we were here. I saw the zedonk yesterday—zedonk is what they're called, a zebra-donkey cross. She seemed gentle but nervous, which is not a shock."

I could not believe my ears. There was a "zedonk" here? There was an animal called a zedonk, first of all. This was stunning information unto itself. A zedonk sounded more like a mythical creation lifted from the pages of *Doctor Dolittle* or *Alice's Adventures in Wonderland* than a real-life occurrence. Moreover, this real-life occurrence was living here, with me? I was living with a zedonk? Clearly, I was more than merely delinquent in my hosting duties; I was ignorant about significant developments.

"I don't know what Emmet is going to do with the animals. It makes me feel ill, if I'm being completely honest. Plus, I think he has a responsibility to the people who work here. Some of them have been here for decades. He says, 'Business is business.' It's ridiculous. He sounds like my father."

Jessica looked puzzled. I was certainly puzzled.

"I don't know what you mean," she said.

"Oh, sorry. I thought you knew. Uncle Ralph left this place to Emmet."

Jessica's mouth opened a little. "To Emmet? He left this place to Emmet?" She placed extra emphasis on "this place."

Lucy nodded.

"Emmet Harrington, that guy over there?" She pointed to Emmet, who was currently standing on a chair doing some sort of weird movements for a circle of partygoers who were laughing.

"The one and only."

"Ralph didn't leave it to your mother?"

Lucy shook her head. "Some money, but not this place."

"How is your brother going to manage an entire estate? Doesn't he have another year at Yale?"

Lucy nodded. She reached over to me and rubbed my neck. Her face was stoic, but I could feel her tension even through the gentleness of her touch. Her tension, her anger, and, simultaneously, her lack of surprise.

Out of nowhere, I was pushed from behind. I fell, then was submerged. My entire body was surrounded by water. Everything was muffled. I felt heavy and yet completely weightless. I was sinking. I held my breath. There were blurred sounds and shapes above, a lot of commotion, but I could discern none of the words. I kept dropping.

My feet touched hard ground. I had reached the bottom. I began to move my legs frantically. I hated this feeling and needed it to stop. A rush of water moved towards me, and I was no longer alone. Lucy was in the water. She was trying to lift me. She struggled to find the right angle. With her hands on either side of me, she was able to move me off the bottom of the pool! But then I sank again and felt a wave of water from above. She had returned to the surface. I began to panic.

Mercifully, the bubbles reappeared as she returned and worked to regrip me. As she lifted, I felt a shift. My body began to pull upwards. Then she released me. I was floating. Lucy swam to the surface again. The sounds above were like waves getting louder. The instant my head surfaced, I took a breath. The moon's rays caressed my face. A crowd had formed at the edge of the pool, and everyone was staring at me.

My first sensation was relief at being able to breathe again. Then I felt the overwhelming urge to get out of the water, but I was suspended there, hanging in place and unable to touch anything stable with my feet. My legs flailed uselessly. I could not even control which direction I faced. My body rotated away from the crowd, and I drifted towards the center of the pool. I was helpless.

I could hear the music.

I focused on Ms. Aretha Franklin's voice. I tried to let myself go, to will my mind to separate from my body, from this horrendous state of utter futility.

Lucy appeared and guided me back to the pool's edge. There was no sloping, gentle incline I could ascend like in the swans' pond. Lucy tried to lift me, straining to get my front end onto the ground above. She had far more trouble now. She was holding on to the side of the pool with one hand and trying to elevate me with the other.

"You monsters who did this, you get in here and help." She was speaking to two of the guys, pointing at them furiously. I say *speaking*, but it was the distinct sound created from the combination of crying and rage.

"I'm not getting in the water," one of them said.

"What is wrong with you?" she screamed. I have never heard her embody and externalize such anger.

"I'll help," one of the splashy young men from earlier said. "We're already wet." He gestured to the other. They slid into the pool, got on either side of me, and lifted. I retreated into myself.

"This thing is really heavy."

I heard splashes, then felt more hands. I was raised up, and then my belly connected with hard ground. I stayed inside myself.

"Here, Lucy," a male voice said.

"I don't want your fucking help," she replied.

"Whoa, whoa. Take it easy."

People inquired about Lucy. "That was weird," someone offered. "I thought turtles were from the ocean," another said. Then the conversations became quieter. The music was turned up on the far side of the pool.

"You okay, Luce?" It was Emmet. I did not hear a reply from Lucy. Perhaps she responded by nodding. She could have just as easily shaken her head.

"Are you okay?" This was Jessica's voice. Still no verbal response. Maybe Lucy shrugged.

I emerged from within myself just enough to see Lucy, her hair and dress drenched. Everyone else had moved on. She looked at me with an expression I cannot describe. Despite my robust vocabulary, no adjective is accurate, or sufficient. She sat beside me for some time in silence and gazed up at the moon. Then she stood up and walked to the residence. I went through the learning pod and lay down underneath a cluster of dense ferns. I could still hear the music and party antics, but they were quieter, now background noise.

I checked in with my whole body. My belly felt tender, presumably scraped when I was pushed from behind. All other parts of me seemed functional. I could smell the water as though it were inside me.

I was furious. Angry at my body and its inability to navigate out of that horrific situation. I had sunk. I had dropped like a rock, then I had floated around like a useless blob. Why was I not equipped with the necessary parts and abilities to flee? Why had I placed myself beside the pool in the first place? I had just been hovering there, right by the edge, completely exposed. Why had I been oblivious to people approaching from behind? I should have known. The fury surged through me, and then there was darkness.

• • •

What I remember next were the sounds of the hose and Lucy's voice somewhere nearby. She was speaking with Michio. The sun was beating down, yet I felt no urge to march towards them and solicit a cooling soak from the hose. My body was already cold. Everything from the night before came rushing back.

I stayed hidden among the ferns and fell back asleep.

I did not awaken until the golden hour was beginning to arrive. I did not feel rested; I felt blurry and foggy. I fell back asleep.

The following sun (maybe? How many suns passed is unclear), I saw Lucy walking away from the pool, past the cages, and towards the forest. Part of me wanted to be whisked away to our forest sanctuary too. I remained in place, numb. I do not know if she was looking for me or retracing her own memories of this place, seeking comfort in spaces where she had experienced joy. She was upset. She had been wronged. She was the one who truly loved this place, not Mother, and certainly not Emmet. She should be the one to be responsible for these lands, these gardens and grasses and forests, the cactuses and flowers, the ponds, the birds and other animals for whom this place was home, whether we chose it or were brought here against our will.

I felt furious again, but this time it was different. Lucy was being denied her rightful place at the helm of this place. That made me angry. And I was mad at the people who had pushed me into the water. I had been part of polite conversation. I had been enjoying the night with Lucy and Jessica. I had every right to be by the edge of the pool or wherever I chose to be.

Lucy walked back from the forest and around the pool's smaller outbuildings on the far side. There were a few scattered people around. Emmet and a girl were seated beside the pool. The radio was playing some gentle music I could not immediately place.

Maybe Lucy was actually looking for me. Even though she had

been wronged, it was possible that she had concern and room in her heart for me. In that moment, I rose up. There was a practical need to stretch, for I had been immobilized for an unknown but extended period of time, but more significantly, I wanted to reach her. I marched through the learning pod. The song on the radio came into focus. I had heard it before, but now I was hearing it differently.

"Freedom. Oh yeah, freedom."

Lucy was on the far side, but saw me approaching. We locked eyes.

Suddenly the music stopped and was replaced by a male voice.

"Senator Robert Francis Kennedy died at 1:44 a.m. today."

Lucy turned to the radio.

"With Senator Kennedy at the time of his death were his wife, Ethel; his sisters Mrs. Stephen Smith and Mrs. Patricia Lawford . . ."

"What?" Emmet said.

The young woman started to cry, and Emmet hugged her. Lucy sat down on the ground and looked around, stunned.

"I just saw him," she said. "I was just talking to him at the campaign office." She dropped her head into her hands.

I was not sure what to do. Sadness radiated from them all. I was about to reach Lucy and considered halting in place out of consideration for the intense emotions they were experiencing, but something compelled me to keep moving. I arrived beside her to show my support. When she looked at me, she burst into tears.

Swan Music

THE NEXT PERIOD was full of human emotion. Various groups of young people arrived, but these were not the same ones who had been over for Emmet's party. These seemed to be Lucy's guests. There was so much sorrow. No one swam or danced. There was occasional laughter, but it would transform into crying. They hugged each other and made toasts to Robert/Bobby using the second person (*you*), as though he were still here or could hear them. There was more sadness during these suns than there had been following Ralph's death. I did not know these people, but my heart reached out to them. Physically, I stayed nearby but kept my distance.

The only time I approached was in a quiet moment and it had a singular purpose. The guests had created an area with photos, signs, and candles in jars, and I wanted to observe this ritual, something I had not been privy to before. As soon as I saw the pictures, I recognized the man. He had been here. He had been here for the traveling symphony and swan dancers. He had smiled when he noticed me.

There was a quiet sun and moon, then Mother arrived, followed later by Father. Cake was brought out in the golden hour, and I realized why. I needed to be part of this and felt it was acceptable for me to join the hub of activity, which still had a somber tone, despite being the most special of occasions: Lucy's birthday. I stood near her, and she rubbed my neck.

The next day she emerged from the residence before the sun had reached its peak and took a gentle stroll around. The air was warm but not hot, and I stepped out into the light so she could find me easily on her way back. She saw me yet walked in the direction that ultimately led to the long and windy driveway, not somewhere I frequented. Then she reappeared and presented me with something I had not enjoyed in quite some time: the bright pink flower of the prickly pear cactus. I took it gingerly from her hand and relished the gift.

"Stay strong, dear magical being. You keep surviving. Actually, that's insufficient. May you be filled with and surrounded by joy."

In that moment, I did not properly understand her words. I knew what they meant on the surface, of course, but their deeper meaning was elusive. She blew me a kiss as she walked away. She did not reemerge. No one did. The pool area was eerily quiet. As time stretched out without Lucy's appearance, an unsettled air settled in. The place was out of balance.

I needed to take action and finally made the decision to address that which was overdue. The instant I saw the violet rays that begin to dance even before the sun begins its ascent, I set off. Due to my intense focus and brisk pace, buttressed by both a cooler temperature and a nice breeze, I arrived in the mammalian section before the sun had reached its peak. The new(ish) arrivals did not notice me initially. Michio was just leaving the area carrying a sprinkler. I paused for a sojourn in a puddle it had created, which would quickly be gone, the water absorbed by thirsty soil.

"Daisuke, look at you out all the way over here," he said as he walked away.

I marched onwards and turned my attention to the residents. Zedonk looked similar to the other brown donkey yet had striped legs and pointier ears. They both noticed me as I got closer, and Zedonk stood on alert, as did Alpaca, who promptly headed in my direction, her neck bobbing as she walked. She was an orangey-er shade of brown. Atop Alpaca's head was a generous poof, and two pronounced teeth stretched skyward from the bottom of her mouth. She really was quite fetching. She studied me as I arrived at the fence, seemed pleased, and then meandered along. Zedonk was still on alert, while Donkey had a calmer presence. He opened his mouth and the most delightfully bizarre song emerged, a series of staccato honking sounds, a full verse of them, which I cherished as a wonderful greeting. Zedonk said nothing but kept watching me. I hoped she would soon understand that I was the absolute opposite of a source of concern.

Gradually, Zedonk moved closer. I held myself in place but also wanted her to see all of me, so stood up. She snorted and hopped back, but then approached again. I stepped forward so that my body was immediately adjacent to the fence. Donkey strolled over and walked in front of Zedonk, sending another glorious honking song out into the world, the very embodiment of an obscure trumpet. This seemed to be the encouragement Zedonk needed to muster enough courage to meet me. She stretched out, reaching under the fence, snorted once more, then touched my nose with hers. It was a lovely act of faith.

I parked myself in a shaded spot outside their enclosure, where I remained for the subsequent suns and moons to welcome these fine beings, show my support, and learn more about them. Another unusual sound drifted through the air periodically, and I intended to determine its source, in due course, when polite to do so. Alpaca and Donkey both enjoyed naps and would even lie down to doze for short periods of time. Zedonk did not. In fact, Zedonk seemed tense. Zebras lived on the African continent—this I had learned from Mr. Williams very early on—while donkeys were more dispersed. I was not even sure where their actual homeland was located. I began to wonder how zedonks came to be, where Zedonk was from, and how she specifically came to be here, in this place. Did anyone call her kind zonkeys?

I pictured Mr. Williams's globe. Zedonk's homeland was on the other side of it. That would certainly explain why she did not seem able to properly relax. She would graze, and she and Donkey gently chewed on each other's neck simultaneously, a marvelous gesture of reciprocity and communion I could only interpret as affectionate or perhaps functional, ideally both. But despite my efforts to disseminate a sense of calmness, Zedonk continued to refrain from partaking in recumbent naps and conveyed an overall sense of anxiousness.

The strange quasi song sailed through the air once again, and I felt compelled to investigate further. I set off in its direction through a denser tree line towards the swans' pond. They seemed well. One was picking at the ground near the shore with their beak while the other floated on the water. They were now joined by frogs, absolutely magnificent individuals and talented musicians in their own right, comfortable both beside the water and immersed in it. Then suddenly, the strange sound was back. The frogs were silent. The sound was originating from the swans.

It was not a song, exactly, or at least not what you would typically call a song. It was some sort of fusion of a wail and a honk, but still musical in an unusual sort of way. The swans were normally peaceful individuals. They had not made these sounds before; I was quite certain of that. This melody was a melancholic soundtrack for the uncertain situation in which we were all enmeshed. Ensnared.

Unvain Waiting

I WAITED ANXIOUSLY for Lucy's return, or even Emmet's. For my egg-laying impulse. For rain.

It was cooler than normal, which was a minor miracle, but there was a dryness in the air and the soil; the entire energy of the place was parched. Michio had to spend more time working to sustain floral life as a result. I was glad he remained. I was unsure what exactly would happen when Emmet returned, however. There were few people around and Michio was my only human constant.

My eggs arrived first. They were preceded, as always, by the need to move across and away, to the one spot in this place that felt sufficiently quiet, dark, and remote. The journey afforded me ample time to engage in deep reflection, and I pondered the meaning of ownership. He (whomever the first proprietor or proprietors had been, then Ralph, then Emmet) owned not only the buildings but also the trees, the soils, the flowers, the plants, the bushes, and the ponds. Moreover, he owned us, or at least those of us who could not simply fly or scamper away. We were beholden to the proprietor, to their (his) decisions, whether made sagely or hastily, selfishly or with a commitment to shared well-being. A similar pattern was true for those whose livelihoods revolved around caring for this place. I began to contemplate the deeper implications of survival, in all its forms, and especially the vulnerability of being dependent on a singular other, a mortal human, and even more than that, a mercurial young man named Emmet who had shown little regard for this place and those within it.

As I laid my eggs, I thought about them, quite literally. I considered them a part of me but also separate. Nothing ever came of them. More specifically, no one ever came out of them. The birds laid eggs too. They would carefully select the locations, methodically collect the most suitable building materials, construct intricate and elaborate structures to house their eggs, and diligently guard their creations. Then, sometime later, baby birds would emerge. My eggs never created baby tortoises.

Although I knew I would enjoy the process of teaching a young tortoise all that I had learned and delight in the imparting of my generous gifts on a worthy other, I had no real conscious desire to be a mother, and no physical compulsion other than to deposit the eggs. Yet I was the only tortoise, and this seemed a loss. There was plenty of space. More of us would enrich the place, liven it up, certainly. I began to wonder why the birds kept reproducing their kind, creating more birds who could soar and sing, while I remained solitary. What did they do differently? I did not need to select building materials or erect any kind of structure. Tortoises emerge from the earth; that much I knew from my very earliest memory. We rise up and burst out into the world. I contemplated staying in the vicinity of my eggs for longer, perhaps placing myself above them as the birds do to offer warmth, but this seemed a fool's errand since being too hot is a perpetual tortoise problem. Maybe it was encouragement that was needed if the eggs housed the tiniest of future tortoises.

But upon further reflection, it dawned on me. Many of the birds worked in pairs. Humans like Lucy had two parents. The reason there were no other tortoises was because there were no other tortoises. Despite my lack of interest in being a mother, the implications of this reality weighed heavily. As long as I was the only tortoise, there could be no other tortoises. I would be the only tortoise who ever walked these lands.

I laid my eggs and moved on. There was still no rain.

Summer stretched forward, and there continued to be no humans living here at all. Shaken by the absence of Lucy and the dark philosophy that had enveloped me, I began to wonder whether something significant had occurred to change the very course of this place. I pondered my options: Retreat into the forest sanctuary and lead a quiet life. Relocate to an area like Takeo's favorite pond, where Michio would surely spend more time . . . if Michio were even to continue his employment. Migrate to the mammals' section for an extended period and join them in whatever fate awaited us, making my solidarity and unity with the other residents crystal clear. The swans' pond was an appealing option due to its easy access to cooling properties, yet it was close to the residence, and this might or might not be advantageous depending on who was to be its occupant.

In my earliest explorations, I had taken note of a smaller gate, not the primary and larger one at the end of the winding driveway used by vehicles. This was a gate through which you could enter or exit only on foot. It was how Takeo and presumably now Michio entered and exited. It was really more of a door. I did something I had never done before: I considered walking through that gate myself. I could loiter nearby and in a most inconspicuous manner due to the abundance of foliage and, once it opened, make my move! Yes, I considered flight. Not bird flight, of course, but rather cautious yet expedient tortoise movement in a singular direction: right out of here.

I carefully assessed the possibilities based on the information at hand. I did not care for vehicles and I avoided the driveway for that reason. There were vehicles beyond these walls; I could hear them. I hypothesized that they were even moving more rapidly. I did not doubt my ability to stop traffic, but I was concerned about where exactly I would go once I navigated around the vehicular hazards. Were there grasses? Ponds? Would I be alone or find new friends? Would there be people like Lucy or humans who seemed less pleased by my presence? So much was unknown, and if I fled, I would be abandoning everyone here. Were I to depart, the other residents would lose a trusted and reliable supporter, a consistent and calm presence with whom to face this brewing storm. I could not leave them. They needed me and I them.

I did not take flight. I continued my journey. Still no rain.

Still no new proprietor either. Fall arrived and was replaced by cooler weather. What would have been called the holidays surely took place somewhere, but not near me. I moved lethargically among the mammals, swans, and Michio as he diligently labored to keep the flora alive without assistance from rain.

Flower buds started to peek out cautiously. The heat descended in full force. Then a distinct sound: Trucks began to rumble up and down the driveway. Admittedly, I am not normally an enthusiastic cheerleader for trucks, but I had a good sense of what their arrival meant.

The woman working at the house became more active. Some

men brought a new table for the area immediately behind the residence, which she oversaw. The pool that had become dirty was cleaned. Pool-Cleaning Man was the same individual I had observed previously. We had rarely interacted, yet I had fond memories of him assisting Takeo with my transportation on that revolutionary occasion. He had to spend many days returning the pool to a state of cleanliness, and I stood nearby to lend my support. I felt a glimmer of hope about what this all meant but did not want to preempt the ascertaining of reliable information about the quality of the person who would be arriving with unsubstantiated joy.

A few suns later, a new person arrived at the residence, a man who was not Emmet though similar in age. He spoke with the woman, sat briefly at the new outdoor table behind the residence, and then went back inside. As the sun was beginning its descent, he emerged again wearing a flowing robe I found dazzling. He strolled down to the pool and placed himself on a lounge chair. He seemed very comfortable and as though he planned to stay. Was he the new proprietor? Where was Emmet? Most significantly, where was Lucy?

I continued to inconspicuously observe from a distance, not yet ready to make my presence obvious. The man returned to the pool later the following sun, and then again the next. He placed a new radio and rearranged some of the chairs. The day was especially warm, and he dove into the water with grace, evoking the smooth movements of a swan. He stayed in the water and swayed to the music. I could feel its vibrations and the gentle timbre of its bass. I wanted to hear it all, to know what he was listening to, what he was bringing to this place. I cautiously moved towards the pool, choosing a path with substantial ground foliage as cover. I wanted to listen but was still not ready to be seen.

As I approached, the music stopped. This was most unfortunate timing. But then, from the silence, emerged a woman's voice.

"Birds flying high, you know how I feel."

I felt her words with my whole body. I was transported to the forest and to my homeland and yet simultaneously felt rooted.

"Oooooh."

Horns leaped out and soared through the air.

The man raised his arms up and swayed.

I did not know who he was, his name, or how he had gotten to this place. I was not sure of his views on tortoises or what he would think of me specifically. What I knew was that he had brought this music. He had brought this woman whose voice lifted my spirits to the sky.

That moon, the skies opened up and the land was drenched with rain.

Plus ça Change

ALTHOUGH THE MAN enjoyed the pool area daily, he never ventured beyond its concrete. He walked over to Michio, who was working in the nearby garden, but used the main path and remained on it. The two looked to have a nice conversation that included shared laughter. The new man had a fabulous laugh. It sounded like it emerged from deep within his body and showed no abandon. I could not understand why he would not explore farther, smell the roses, inspect the eucalyptus, admire the swans, marvel at Zedonk and friends. Michio was doing a beautiful job maintaining his grandfather's floral legacy, especially impressive given the extra-dry conditions we had been forced to endure. The new man should want to see this place, to appreciate his new home, in all its glory.

Many questions remained. Did he have a family? Would he have parties?

Where was Lucy?

My state of confusion notwithstanding, I discreetly edged ever closer to this now sanctified pool area, the only space he deemed worthy of his time. I stealthily maneuvered behind the buildings and through the thickest greenery until I was right behind his location. By the time I arrived, he had moved on, but I settled in among some lady ferns against the wall in the shade just around the corner.

I felt shy. It is true. I was nervous about meeting a new person. I had made the acquaintance of Michio and Clara, but that evolved so organically and rapidly, I had done no preparations or strategizing. This was turning into quite a production, and I was working myself into a tizzy. His superb taste in music was encouraging, while his lack of interest in enjoying the full landscapes of this place was perplexing indeed.

"You're all . . ."

He was back.

"I need . . ."

He was singing.

"To get by."

What a lovely voice. It inspired me. I decided to be bold. I edged forward and peeked around the corner. He was in long pants and a shirt now, as well as a stylish hat, reading a newspaper.

I moved myself into the learning pod and then stood like a statue against the wall. The angle of the lounger meant he could not see me directly. He sang a little tune as he read, and I enjoyed the sound of his voice immensely. I edged forward, and it was then that he noticed me. He stared, saying nothing. In that moment, I lay down. Perhaps I sought to make it clear that I was staying, that I was comfortable, that this was my home too.

It rang out into the air, his laugh. He seemed to be delighted. Or shocked. Perhaps a bit of both. In any event, he stared at me and I held his gaze. He shook his head, smiling. He went back to his paper and hummed to himself. Well, technically, he hummed to both of us.

When he finished reading, he sat up, looked over, and chuckled again, then stood up and made his way back to the residence. As the sun began its descent, I contemplated sleeping right there in the learning pod, further establishing my presence, yet something in me felt this was unnecessary. Instead, I opted for comfort and tucked back in among the ferns, ready for a new dawn, a new day, with the distinct sense that my cautious glimmer of hope had been warranted.

When the man did not return throughout the following sun, I had a flicker of self-doubt and worry. But my good sense took over, and I reminded myself that I had done nothing wrong. I had simply shown myself. I knew full well that people were busy. They came and went on different schedules; they had commitments and responsibilities beyond the pool, things to do that made time by the pool possible. He would be back.

The new man emerged during the golden hour, and he was not alone. Two other men were with him, bursting with excitement and glee and gushing over the place, rightfully so. They admired the pool area and wandered off the concrete into the gardens. I found that reassuring, although the arrival of a group of men also elicited more frightening memories. I focused on the possibility that these would be men of honor.

"You are going to love this hi-fi, Richard!" the new proprietor/resident/identity-as-of-then-unconfirmed called to his friend who was studying the stilt-puff trees.

Richard walked towards the hi-fi, this time choosing the side with the learning pod. As he passed, he stopped in his tracks. He had spotted me. His mouth opened.

"Melvin, are you aware that there is a giant turtle?" he said, then to the third man who had meandered off somewhere out of view, he called, "Oh, honey, you need to see this!"

All three stood there in a row looking right at me.

"I mean, wow," Richard said. "Where exactly does a creature like this come from? And how do you move him around? A giant box? Or a limo?"

"I couldn't tell you," Melvin said. "Emmet said there were a lot of animals."

Emmet!

"Animals plural?"

Melvin shrugged. "I guess so. I haven't gone looking."

"Has Emmet been here yet?"

Lucy's brother was still the proprietor!

Melvin shook his head. "Y'all are my first real visitors. I don't know how he's going to manage this, but he says he's going to figure it out."

"If someone offered me a gorgeous white boy who put me up in a mansion and all I had to do was watch over Shelley here, that's a deal I would take."

"Richard," Melvin said.

Richard threw his hands in the air. "Oh, I know, I know, you're in love. But the amenities sure ain't bad." He looked at me. "Come on, Shelley! Let's dance!"

They wandered back to the hi-fi, and a gentle crackle filled the air. She was back.

Her voice took on a new power in the soft gray light of dusk.

"May the lord bless our angel on Earth, Ms. Nina Simone!"

The men had their arms around one another, the horns played, and they sang along, creating a new harmony.

Melvin. Ms. Nina Simone. Shelley.

• • •

Melvin enjoyed the company of his friends, who would come by every now and then. They swam, danced, and listened to music. Melvin had a large collection of records, and my repertoire began to expand significantly thanks to his tastes.

He did not talk to me much but would always say hello and goodbye when I was in the vicinity. He read a great deal, not only newspapers but also books. Sometimes he would hum to himself or sing along with the records and write in a notebook. I appreciated everything about his musicality. Though every day, I still watched and listened for Lucy.

The residence-maintaining woman was the only female who emerged. However, I did finally learn that her name was Eliana after observing up close a conversation she had with Melvin. Her hair was becoming more streaked with silver. We had shared this place for an extended period, yet because her time and efforts focused almost entirely on the residence, we had very infrequently been in the same area. Nevertheless, her presence was reassuring, and I was pleased that she remained.

As I was making my way back from the swans one day, I heard vehicular activity around the residence. The elusive Emmet had finally arrived. He was even more of an adult and the sight was somewhat jarring. His body was larger and his energy different. He was clearly enamored with Melvin and did not even notice me. This new Emmet marched right past the pool carrying a small cage and released the pair of bright yellow birds inside it into one only slightly larger. Emmet and Melvin stood together as the unsettled birds flitted about, trying to understand their new surroundings.

"They still don't sound nearly as good as you," Emmet said to Melvin, squeezing his arm. By turning towards Melvin, Emmet noticed me. "Wow."

Melvin smiled. "You didn't tell me about Shelley."

"Shelley! Oh, that's just about perfect."

"Shelley is great company," Melvin said, chuckling. I was unsure what to interpret from this laughter; I was, unquestionably, great company. "But I'm glad you're finally here."

Emmet set the smaller cage he had been carrying down against the wall, and the two of them walked back to the residence. I tried to wrap my head around this new grown-up Emmet. He was calmer and gentler, or perhaps it was Melvin who brought out a sweeter and lighter side of him.

But I stared at the cages and felt the weight of that lack of change.

Eyes off of You

EMMET DID NOT stay long. The fact that Emmet stayed only briefly appeared to be a source of consternation for Melvin and resulted in a tense conversation. I kept my distance and remained near the cages to support the new captive birds in their transition. I wondered where they had been before. If they had been born free or into cages. They were not particularly vocal, but would sit together and sing quiet songs, and I would lend my strength. Michio was in charge of feeding them, and his company, however brief, was nice, despite the circumstances that brought us together.

Following Emmet's departure, Melvin returned to his reading, writing, singing, swimming routine. He also began to walk around the grounds more, although he did not venture to the far corners by any means. Undoubtedly, exposure to even some of the splendor of this place would be good for him, so this was a promising development. He enjoyed the flowers and colorful gardens the most. One day he carried a chair over from the pool area and set it up facing the birds. My mind summoned the memory of Clara: the sound of her transcendent voice when she would sing to the birds, and, of course, her wondrously dramatic liberatory final gesture. I hoped Melvin might sing to them, at minimum, but he remained silent.

"Howdy, Shelley," he would say to me and then sit quietly, watching the birds' movements pensively. He seemed content, but less exuberant than he had been upon arrival.

One hot day, he emerged earlier than usual, swam, and then came over to the cages to dry off in the direct sun. Michio arrived to place the birds' food, and the two exchanged friendly greetings.

"I'm sorry these birds are another thing for you to worry about," Melvin said.

Michio shook his head. "No, it's no problem at all. There were birds here before."

"What happened to them?"

"Oh, they were released."

"Oh my," Melvin said, glancing at the cages. "How is your wife doing? Ayame, right?"

"That's right. Ayame is well, thank you for asking. Lily, my daughter, is a handful. But Ayame has the patience of . . . well, a tortoise." They both looked over at me, and Melvin laughed theatrically. I was patient. That was correct rather than funny, but I did not believe Melvin meant me any disrespect.

"I would love to see a photo of her, of them both. Whenever you have the chance, you know where to find me." He gestured towards the pool. "Actually, why don't you just bring them here? Would they like to go for a swim? I can clear out, and you and your family can enjoy the pool all to yourselves."

"Oh, no, that is far too kind of you. I would never dare to impose—"

"Nonsense. Don't be silly. This place is much too big for one person."

Michio said nothing. I believe he was shocked.

"I insist. I absolutely insist. I will be offended if you don't. How about this Sunday? I am going out for a big night on the town Saturday anyway and will likely need the entire next day to recover!"

"That is most generous of you, Melvin. I am speechless."

"It's my pleasure."

"We will act with the utmost respect, I assure you. My wife only knows that the owner is often away and that you are a kind man, nothing else."

Melvin became more serious. He nodded. "I'm assuming Emmet pays you extra for your discretion or something like that."

Michio did not reply.

"I'm sorry, that was rude of me. Ayame is such a lovely name, and so is Lily."

"Thank you. *Ayame* means 'iris,' and we joke that it was fate and flowers that brought us together. My grandfather's favorite flower was the lily. He adored them all, and you can see the results of his love every day, but the lilies were his absolute favorite."

Melvin's smile was warm. "What a beautiful legacy you all are."

Michio, Ayame, and little Lily arrived as the sun was halfway to its peak. Michio took such pleasure in showing them many of his favorite places, and Takeo's. Lily was small but boisterous and curious about the world around her. I beamed when Michio introduced me.

"The famous Daisuke. What a pleasure," Ayame said. I was famous!

They had a lovely time in the pool area. The adults helped Lily into the water, and I thought she might scream at the top of her lungs, but instead she seemed mesmerized by this change in her physical environ, the feeling of being enveloped by water rather than air as she floated like her namesake. At one point as they lounged in the shade, Ayame walked over to me with a slice of apple in hand, which I most enjoyed. The days were beginning to get shorter and cooler, but the sun blessed the Yamadas' time with full warmth.

It was one of the last hot days that year, and autumn arrived with more intensity than usual. I did not mind the cooler temperatures one bit, but they meant Melvin spent less time at the pool and then ceased swimming altogether. Whenever he would arrive, he would place himself near the hi-fi, sometimes wrapped in a blanket, and let the music envelop him too. I would move myself closer to share in the musical delights, but due to the absence of conversation resulting from the dearth of guests, I learned less about who exactly I was listening to. This did not prevent me from appreciating the poetry of the lyrics, the joy being shared through song, or the sorrow emanating both vocally and instrumentally.

When he decorated the hi-fi and radio area with red, gold (a lot of gold), and green, I felt certain Emmet would return. I briefly allowed myself to imagine that Lucy, too, would reappear, but somehow, I knew that would not happen.

Instead, Richard and an assorted collection of friends did. Their group had a joyful energy, and I moved myself close to the festive area without entering it, opting instead to remain around the corner. They enjoyed the snacks Melvin had brought down and sang along with a number of the songs.

"My mother called. She was crying," one of the men said.

"Have you heard from your father at all?" Melvin asked.

"Not a word."

"When we said goodbye last time, my father almost hugged me," another man said. "He diverted to, you know, a solid pat of the arm, but it's something."

"My parents came, and we had dinner." This was one of the women. "We all just played along with the roommate thing."

"Hi!" the other woman said with a phony, exaggerated smile. "Hello, roommate."

"Yeah, it wasn't a disaster, though. I don't know, I feel like it was a big thing for them."

"Maybe in a decade they'll get there."

"Oh, you think we're still going to be together in a decade, do you?"

"If you're lucky!"

Everyone laughed.

"It's true, I am a lucky woman."

"Awwwwwwwww," the men all said in unison.

"But no one is as lucky as Carol with her supermom, who is all 'I love you no matter what. Fight the man.'"

"Amen to that." This was Richard, and there was a clinking of glasses.

"To good family and chosen family." More clinking of glasses.

"Ain't that the truth," Melvin said with a note of somberness in his voice.

I took a few more steps towards the gathering and into their view. A woman noticed me first.

"Melvin, oh my god, you were not kidding!"

They all spun around to look at me.

"Ladies and gentle ladies, may I present my associate Shelley," Melvin said. This thoughtful introduction evoked memories of Lucy, happy ones.

The woman who had noticed me approached and yet I did not fear the worst (i.e., a poke). She presented me with a cookie. I was not sure what to make of this item, but I partook. The texture was unusual but the flavor pleasing. "Merry Christmas, Shelley. May all our people be free."

How could anyone disagree with that?

Myriad

AFTER THE ONE seasonal social gathering, this place became extremely quiet as far as human noise was concerned. There was no sign of Eliana or even Michio for that matter. Maybe they were with their families. (I had always found it peculiar that Eliana worked during the "holidays.")

I used this time to reflect on who we are forced to be with, and what allows us to choose who we are connected to. I pondered the meaning of chosen family, with all its intricacies and liberating implications. The absence of tortoises in this place crawled back into my mind but I did not dwell, instead deciding to focus on what I could control—my ability to support those who were here, to serve as a worthy companion and neighbor and friend for them all. I wondered if they thought of me as family.

Once in a while, from the treetops, I would hear a familiar tune, a song that had been sung by the birds previously held in the cages. Maybe some of them had chosen to remain in this place, or to visit periodically to see how we were doing, possibly even to inquire after me. That would be magnanimous.

I decided to check on the swans and mammals. Yet instead of beginning the journey in the usual way by weaving well around the giant stone structure known as the residence, I did something bold: I went directly towards it.

This audacious decision was animated by an interesting combination of factors, a veritable bricolage of emotions and impetuses, if you will. My sustained avoidance of the residence had been rooted in the blatant unkindness of the broom-wielding man. Yet it had been an extremely long time by human standards since I had laid eyes on him. I was using my apprehension about him and his tarnishing of the path to the residence as an excuse. In fact, I had been restricting my own ideas of what was possible. I had the right to not only be here but also walk near the residence if I so chose.

"R-E-S-P-E-C-T," I sang to myself, Ms. Franklin's voice both pushing and pulling me along. I was traversing a border, the precipice between the thoroughly human domain and the rest of this place with all its multispecies glory, both literal and figurative.

"Good morning, Daisuke," I heard, out of nowhere, as Michio walked past me towards the back of the residence and then out of view.

I maintained my focus, which had ascended into determination. A cool breeze from behind encouraged me. Was I unsettling what were simply my own impositions and inhibitions, or had my mind been following the requisite order of things? How do we decide what is possible for ourselves, and for others? Are these divisions a reflection of the very limitations of time and space, or are barriers created, structured into the fibers of our conscious minds, and reaffirmed by the architectural choices of those who employ architects? Those who are able to employ architects, that is.

Yet birds are architects too.

This was a complicated sociological and philosophical puzzle.

"You're on a mission." Michio was back from wherever he had

been. I was. I was indeed. I remained steadfast as I reached the outer edge of the residence, an even deeper sense of exhilaration burning inside me, fuel for this rebel quest, my most intrepid journey yet.

The patio behind the residence was now in view. The table and chairs. Giant pots of flowers. Another fountain, albeit a small one. As I got closer, I realized that despite my now indefatigable resolve, there was a problem. Actually, at least five of them. Stairs. I had never seen them up close (due to you-know-who-who-shall-remain-unnamed, never to be mentioned again).

Whether due to the gust of wind that danced behind and under me, or the strength of my convictions, I forged on. There were not five steps—there were ten. Below them was the patio area in all its human-constructed, human-oriented majesty, supplemented only strategically by foliage (which was, admittedly, robust and striking). But these stairs came between me and all that jazz.

I studied the dimensions of the stairs to determine if I could traverse them, one at a time. I considered trying to slide but foresaw only pain. How had Clara navigated Ralph around when he needed a wheelchair and her assistance? Goodness, whoever had designed this place had not even thought about the barriers for other people, let alone tortoises.

I surveyed the immediate environment, desperately looking for alternatives. And there, right in front of my lovely face, was the solution. The stairs were built into a hill. Beside the stairs, there was a hill covered in grass. It was a sharper angle than the slope I had successfully descended many times to be among the rocks for the night of explosions, but not dramatically so. I felt confident I could manage. And I did.

I sang to myself as I stepped onto this new terrain and examined it from up close. The ground was covered in an elaborate series of carefully placed stones, essentially art in the ground. The fountain was bigger than it had looked from afar. The table was elevated, up a series of five other steps that were farther apart. Their spacing created a graduated effect, one I might even be able to navigate if there were reason for me to be beside this table. Reason or desire.

I had achieved something monumental by pushing my thinking and body in new, deeper directions. This journey had required both physical and intellectual prowess. I felt triumphant, yet also sleepy. My eyelids were heavy, and I drifted into slumber.

I was suddenly awakened by Emmet's voice. He was directing two men who were wheeling a large wooden crate. When they reached the top of the stairs, they lifted it by hand and carried it down.

"Where do you want it?" one of them called.

"How about by the fountain."

The men placed this crate on the ground and unlocked the latches but left it closed. One of them noticed me as they left but oddly did not react in any way. Melvin appeared through the large glass doors revealing a feeling of uncertainty, one I shared.

Emmet stood in front of the crate and spread his arms wide, facing Melvin.

"Surprise! Aren't you gonna come see what I got you?"

"Honey, you're too late for Christmas and too early for Valentine's Day."

"Bull feathers! I don't need holidays telling me what to do when it comes to you."

Melvin tentatively descended the steps towards Emmet.

"Speaking of feathers . . ." Emmet turned around, opened the crate, and then stepped back. A blue face peered out, topped by a delicate crown, almost as though flowers were emerging from this individual's head.

"What on earth?" Melvin said. Emmet was smiling from ear to ear.

The new arrival burst out of the crate and stopped about

three tortoise lengths in front of it. This was a bird. A substantially sized bird. His neck was a stunningly vibrant shade of regal blue. He looked around, taking everything and everyone in, and then opened his mouth. As you know, I pride myself on being melodically open-minded, on listening for the unique beauty in even the most unusual music. Well, this was most unusual indeed. The sound that emerged was like a wail, but with swagger. The bird hopped right up onto the fountain and took a drink.

"You got me a peacock?"

Gems

AS WINTER TURNED to spring and then to summer and the heat came back with renewed intensity, Emmet visited (is it technically visiting when you are the proprietor?) approximately once every thirty suns and he would only ever stay briefly. He hosted discussions around the pool that Melvin would not attend. I would make myself scarce as well, for these seemed serious in nature, although Emmet still laughed at least a few times and became the showy and blustery version of himself I had known for so long. Eliana would bring drinks, but these gatherings were decidedly more work than party.

Meanwhile, Peacock wandered from his initial placement behind the residence to pretty much wherever he wanted. Of course, the free animals came and went of their own accord, but other than the cat given to Ralph whom I rarely saw even initially (and who completely disappeared into the night not long afterwards), we had not had another resident who was permitted to roam as they pleased other than me. I had mixed views about this turn of events, not because I felt others should be denied the right to freedom of movement; quite the contrary. I knew nothing of Peacock's story, so was uncertain about whether this was somewhere he wanted to be, even with the ability to move about here, there, and everywhere.

He was confident, however; that I can say with certainty. He would wander around the residence, the pool area (including *on* the tables, if you can believe it!), Takeo's favorite pond, wherever the spirit moved him, and he never faced reproach, nor did it even seem to occur to him that there might be restrictions on his mobility or patterns of decorum to respect. He would sing, seemingly at random, especially in the spring. After a while, it became almost like background noise, an obscure horn blaring in the distance. I believe the sonic offering was Peacock's own version of the daily recognition chant, albeit one he felt compelled to share six or seven times a day, and without anyone to respond in-kind. As a result, it was a one-way announcement, and the rest of us were its involuntary recipients. "Oh, Peacock is by the residence." "He is among the swans." "On this side now, over by the hi-fi." "And he's back on the table."

The richness and depth of his hue gave him a jewellike quality. And there was the matter of his tail. *Tail* is a wholly inadequate word for what Peacock possessed. It included not only splashes of regal blue but also beaming green and shimmering yellow. When he felt so moved, he would fan out this extraordinary and intricate interweaving of colors, a true work of bodily art, for all to behold. This often happened when there was an audience that piqued his interest, especially a human one. However, when he first made my acquaintance, he was sufficiently impressed to deem me worthy of a full display, which is not particularly surprising given my unquestionably impressive shape and size but pleasing nevertheless.

At first, I do not believe he registered me as someone, and on his first pass near the cages where I had been resting, he paid me no mind at all. When he retraversed the area, I was up and taking turns stretching each of my legs. He stared at me for a good long while by peacock standards, tilting his head, and then poof, up with the magic.

Emmet's meetings were Peacock's favorite audience for his bodily tableau. He would spot the men, wail, stroll in their direction, casually mill about, and then BOOM. The men were always impressed. I felt quite certain I would elicit a similar reaction; however, as noted earlier, I opted to keep my distance from these gatherings and the showy version of Emmet. I preferred the Emmet who would appear around Melvin.

Regardless of who he was around, Melvin seemed to be changing in a range of noteworthy ways. One day as I approached the mammals' quadrant, I observed him holding Donkey. Another man was filing Donkey's feet! A most interesting set of developments also began to occur on the pool side of this place. (*Interesting* is a wholly inadequate adjective but I am trying to maintain a modicum of restraint, to keep my cool, if you will.) Melvin also began to host more regular small gatherings and diversified the guests. Many of the people who had visited us for Christmas whom I had found to be amiable would return, and I always enjoyed their company. But other groups started coming too, and I am overjoyed to share that many of them were musical. Not only did they enjoy listening to music, but they created their own melodies and harmonies! Some brought instruments! Not harps or large drums, but many guitars and some smaller percussion options.

Melvin began to add decor around the pool, like the items that had been brought out for special occasions in the past, but these were permanent additions. New chairs and couches. Large potted flowers. Lights. Oh, the lights twinkled like our own personal ceiling of stars, the beloved offspring of the full sky that gleamed and blinked above Melvin's strategically placed beacons. He succeeded in creating an environment that was thoughtfully welcoming and designed for sharing, for collaboration. There were still spaces for quiet solitary reflection or paired symbiosis and affection, yet alongside them was a greater sense of inclusivity, one explicitly crafted.

Musical people began to come by more often in groups of two or four, and even sometimes five or six, and Melvin would join them, offering his voice, or ideas, or both. I would put myself as close as possible to the musical action, ideally right in the center of it. I marveled at the process of creation, at the subtle and more significant changes in chords and tempo, the dramatic pauses that were added, presumably the direct result of my presence. Oh, how I love a dramatic pause. You linger in it, wondering, Whatever will come next?

One day, a piano was wheeled out and given a prominent location in the hearth of Melvin's space. When he sat down and began to play, I felt its music deep within me. The sound moved my spirit, the range, the exceptional intricacy of what a single instrument could send forth into the world! I parked myself right beside the piano whenever there was a musical crowd, for I could not get enough.

In contrast, Emmet was not initially persuaded.

"By the pool? An entire piano?"

"The sound out here is beautifully clear and crisp," Melvin replied.

"I don't doubt that, but by the pool? You play by the pool?"

"I do, and friends come by and play too."

Emmet paused before replying, seemingly pondering the deeper meaning of the words. "A lot of different friends?"

"Good people, Emmet. There is nothing to worry about."

Melvin brought the piano to life with a delicate yet fierce interweaving of melancholy and hope. Emmet stared at me. As his eyes filled with tears, I did not look away.

• • •

Both Melvin's and Emmet's gatherings around the pool continued unabated and yet never intersected. I knew this was not by coincidence and suspected it required careful planning. Some of Emmet's meetings took advantage of Melvin's redesign, and the stocky men in business suits provided a stark visual contrast to the lithe and long-haired musical aficionados.

This ebb and flow was a consistent pattern, and multiple Christmases came and went with only minimal fanfare, and without Emmet. Emmet's meetings and visits both became even more infrequent, while Melvin's musical extravaganzas continued at full pace, much to my utter delight.

Then I witnessed a most unexpected gathering beside the pool, one with Melvin, Eliana, and Michio.

"People love coming here, so why not formalize it?" Melvin said. "I will still host friends and keep some things chill, but for those I don't know, they should pay. It seems the logical next step."

"A business?" Michio asked.

Melvin nodded. "Maybe a sliding scale depending on if they want to stay for longer, and how much they have. You know what I mean—the struggling ones just pay the minimum, but those with means, well, we can give them the premium package. This is not unreasonable for what we offer. We'll split the proceeds equally."

Eliana and Michio looked shocked.

"No, that doesn't seem fair," Michio said. "You are the musical genius. Well, and Eliana, she does so much. She deserves more than me."

"This isn't just about music, it's about an entire experience. We all contribute."

"What does Mr. Harrington think about this?" Eliana asked.

"You don't need to worry about that. I will tell him when the time is right."

Melvin stood up, selected a specific record, took out the liner notes, and read aloud: "Our deepest thanks to Melvin Green for a depth of understanding and brilliance the likes of which we have never seen." He raised his eyebrows. "And to Shelley for the patience."

Eliana and Michio looked at me, then back at Melvin.

"There is a line between generosity and exploitation," he said. "And there is a time for knowing your worth."

This was a significant amount of information for one humble tortoise to process all at once. There were going to be even more musicians. Melvin was transforming this into a proper music house. And I had been recognized in a record!

Eighth Wonder

LITTLE CHANGED FROM my vantage point, not being one privy to matters like payments. But musical people began staying for longer than a single evening, and certain groups were with us for many suns and moons. They would eat behind the residence or around the pool or even take their food off to quieter areas in the shade or sun. I appreciated the additional fruit offerings that resulted from their dispersal, and I have no doubt the beauty of this place inspired even richer creative introspection and expression.

There were some boisterous social events, including two album release parties. But most of the time, Melvin kept the number of people in this place at a single time reasonable, which allowed him to focus more on the details of their music and lyrics, and how we could help sculpt them into even more evocative shapes.

Music was both work and enjoyment for me given my crucial role as muse. Among the guests, there was a politeness range, or continuum, you might say, and some seemed awfully fond of the sound of their own voices (not only when singing but also while talking). These ones were more resistant to Melvin's ideas. Others clearly relished their time here in all its facets. One temperamental man had a tantrum that included tossing a tambourine at me. I was physically unscathed yet still certifiably unimpressed, particularly due to my sincere appreciation for the tambourine.

"Lee, that sort of behavior is not welcome here," Melvin said. "If you do it again, I'm afraid you will have to leave." I beamed with pride.

One night when there were no musicians, Richard and Melvin lounged around the pool drinking. Melvin was happy. He seemed surer of himself and confident. I listened to their conversation and to the music. The quality brought by the hi-fi was undeniable. The records offered texture and depth of sound, the next best thing to real-life musicians. I gained greater understanding of the artists through sustained listening, even those I had not met in person and supported directly. I wondered where they had honed their craft and who their muses were. Were any of my relatives also assisting musicians? The answer was simply unknowable.

"I mean, all of this is incredible, Mel. I love seeing you getting some well-deserved respect."

"I appreciate that, man. Really, I mean it. In some ways I can't believe how well it's going, but it's about the people, right? Surround yourself with good people and keep working. That's all you can do." Melvin took a drink. "How's life in LA these days?"

"You know, ups and downs. My students are feeling it all, the good and the bad."

"What a time to be a teenager."

"No doubt. I almost forgot to tell you—I saw some live music last week. Great guitarist, and the white girl who was singing, she really has her own thing going on. She looks like she could get blown away by the wind, but then her voice, I've never heard one like it. They were just hanging round after, so I told her about you.

Maybe she'll get in touch. Speaking of, have you considered renaming this place?"

Melvin laughed. "Oh, what, Chilton Manor isn't doing it for you? Not really capturing the essence of what we're building?"

"Emmet didn't want to change the name?"

"Definitely not. Flying low and all that jazz. I guess you could say I've taken a different approach."

"How about Green Records?"

"Ha! I think that's getting a bit ahead of ourselves."

Richard looked around. "Harmony Heaven? New Eden?"

"King and Queen Ranch?"

They howled with laughter.

"Shelley's Songland."

It was good alliteration, if I do say so myself.

While I spent more time around the pool and quite literally in the center of many of the musical gatherings (only three people tried to play me like a drum), I did not neglect my duties to the other residents. The mammals' enclosure had been expanded, a worthy renovation that gave them more room to move and eat, although they remained confined within fences. Some suns they would be permitted to access the whole, new full range. At other times, one area would be closed off, allowing the grasses to grow back with more thickness. This seemed like sound logic to me, although I wondered whether the mammals would prefer to simply roam all around this place as Peacock and I did. There could be safety concerns with that arrangement, though, for the residents and the humans alike. The mammals would need to learn about vehicles and not to drink from the pool. (Would they want to swim? That was a mystery.) They would, undoubtedly, ingest flora that Michio (and

Takeo) had invested a significant amount of labor into sustaining and beautifying. This would be distressing for Michio and could lead to some gardens being irreparably damaged. I could also picture Zedonk feeling skittish around the sometimes-erratic energy and sounds of the musicians and her movements becoming frenetic. On balance, I concluded that while this was a proper music house, the mammals were probably safest with some limitations on their movements.

While I continued to avoid the front of the residence, I would travel all along its back during my journeys to and from the pool. Particularly at the outset, this route was enlivening. The act of crossing into what had for so long been sacrosanct due simply to its position as a residence for humans was perhaps insignificant for Peacock but caused a wee flurry in my belly. I would confidently move across the patio, feeling no pressure to depart or adjust my speed. If I were so inclined, I could pause and admire the area and the intricate rock artwork in the ground or peer through the giant glass doors to see if there was any movement of interest inside the residence. I felt empowered.

During one especially vibrant sun descension, I was strolling from the residence patio right down the main path to the pool when I spotted a new group of musicians. They were wandering around and marveling at the place. By the time I arrived, the golden hour was in full effect and the musicians had settled in. I walked with aplomb towards the hearth to reclaim my place in its center and see what this group had to offer. I do not remember anything initially striking about the men, but there was a woman, and she summoned my attention immediately. There was something about her energy that captivated me. It was hard to describe, which is really saying something given my robust vocabulary. She was singing, and I marched with decided purpose until I was directly in front of her. We locked eyes, and her face expanded into a smile. Her voice was like a bell and a storm simultaneously. She reminded me of Lucy. They likely would have been around the same age.

"Who is this extraordinary creature?" she asked when the song wrapped up. One of the men immediately started talking about what he wanted to change in the song's bridge, but Melvin gave her (and me) the courtesy of a response.

"This is Shelley," he said before turning his attention to the man's comment.

She sat down directly in front of me. "Well, I've never known anyone like you."

The men kept debating, with one proposing alternate chords on his guitar. She kept admiring me and I her.

"I like that slightly disjointed feel, right before the chorus comes in. To show the contrast," Melvin said.

"Like you're lost but then you get your bearings. The feeling of being abandoned, followed by this realization of your solitude, this acceptance of your new identity or renewed sense of self," she said. Her song was my own.

The other singing man in her band barely registered what she had said and played a new series of chords.

"I want to try it with a capo on the second fret," he said, gesturing for her to stand up with his hands. She did not. He started to play, and his sheer musical talent equaled hers, that was clear. Her eyes held mine as her voice flowed. She was my spring.

At one point, the discussion became very focused on the guitars, and she moved to a quieter chair nearby with a notebook in hand. I followed and positioned myself at her side. As she wrote, she would gaze up at the sky or the trees in the distance, or at me and smile. Then write some more.

The musicians who visited our proper music house varied in talent, and some were truly exceptional. Yet of all the people who graced the edges of our waters with their creativity, their poetry, the magic created by their voices, hands, and spirits, she was the most exquisite.

"Stay with me a while, baby," she sang to me.

I awakened the instant the sun began to rustle and stretch, hoping that hers would be an overnight band and she would be back. Alas, it was not, and she did not return. I had grown well accustomed to managing my disappointment, but the realization that she was gone did set me back.

I moped. I admit that I moped. Emotional management is an intricate skill, and despite the plethora of practice I have had, this does not mean I never waver. Moreover, I am not sure that an inauthentic state of unwavering pleasantry would be advisable. Perpetual positivity seems to have its own flaws.

In a dejected state, I slept under a tree for a few moons before wandering up the gentle slope in the direction of the forest, feeling that its embrace would comfort and then lift me. Yet the sound of the piano arrested my steps as it filled my heart. The piano alone can elevate and animate me in profound ways, but in this instance, it was not simply the music; it was also the voice. She had returned!

I surely do not need to tell you how expediently I turned right around and shuffled my pretty little self all the way to the majesty at that piano. Melvin played. She sat on the bench beside him like she was resting on a cloud, singing. Upon noticing me, her face lit up like the moon at its fullest. The two were painting an entire sky.

Melvin transitioned into a beautiful song of his own creation. She nodded along, smiling, then stood up and twirled. Melvin beamed and swayed as he played, and she spun with her arms outstretched. I wanted time to stretch out infinitely.

When the song ended, they positioned themselves in some of

Melvin's softest chairs and he opened a bottle of wine. "Let's get this party started!" she said. I most certainly repositioned myself as they clinked glasses.

"Above and beyond anything I feel about him personally, his talent and vision, his musical ferocity, they're incredible," she said. "He's like you in that way, but you're a bit humbler!" She laughed.

"He's exceptional. You are quite a pair. You need a worthy band."

She paused, then nodded. "I don't need to tell you how tough it is out there."

"Oh, I hear you, mama. I hear you. You need an ambitious group so you can spread your wings, vocally and lyrically. I think you'll find one—or one will find you."

"There is a British drummer who has been listening to our record, apparently. There's even a woman in the band already. I don't know if anything will come of it."

"Interesting! See, now that doesn't surprise me. Maybe it'll be the one. I could see a solo career in your future too."

"I don't know about that."

"How many songs do you have?"

"A lot. Basically, a treasure chest full."

"I bet it's got treasure, all right. I wish I could produce you myself."

"Is that the direction you're headed?"

"Oh, I don't know. Still to be determined. I need the right opportunity. We'll see. A wise woman once observed that it's tough out there."

The sun was beginning its descent and creating a soft pink glow that enveloped her. A scratching sound above us caught everyone's attention. I could not believe my eyes. Peacock. Peacock was on the roof of the learning pod! He wailed at his highest volume, then spread out every single beaming feather in his tail.

"Oh my! He likes you!"

"I feel so flattered. Thank you, fine sir!" she called.

Peacock was right pleased with himself and paraded around.

"Does he go up there often?"

"First time. I hope he doesn't try that up at the house!"

"Hold on," she sang, her voice bursting out into the world. "The night is coming and the peacock flew for days." She laughed. "That might need a rewrite."

"And he certainly cannot!"

"No? They don't fly?"

"It's more of a running, fluttering sort of fiasco."

"How did he get up there? That's gotta be at least twelve feet."

"Clearly you have inspired him."

She smiled, took a drink, and looked at me. She reached forward and rubbed my neck. "You know, Shelley, you look like a Sara to me."

I never saw her again, but she was always with me. I heard her many, many times. She soared.

Darwinian

MY MIND WAS more or less occupied depending on how many musical discoveries there were to be made and what else was going on that required my supervision. But I always wondered about Lucy. I did not count how many hundreds of suns had passed since I had seen her, maybe thousands. Other than this empty gulf in my heart, everything seemed to be progressing smoothly, until one crisp evening.

Melvin was sharing his usual incisive understanding with a group of three musicians. I found their sound pleasant but not remarkable, so had taken leave for pre-slumber pensive reflections. Michio and his family had stopped by not long before, and Lily looked to have at least doubled in size. I had not witnessed the growth of a human from tiny to small before, so was pondering the pace at which she had both physically and mentally grown.

Then, from behind me, I heard someone arriving. It was Emmet, and he was not walking in his usual manner, but rather with more of a shuffle. He had never before set foot at the pool area when Melvin had musical guests. Not once.

Melvin spotted him promptly from afar.

"Will you excuse me for a moment? Please, just keep working through that one. I think there's potential there," Melvin said, and he moved through the learning pod lounge with such alacrity. The interception occurred before Emmet made it into the pool area. Melvin walked right up to Emmet and grabbed him, more to hold him up than embrace him.

"I didn't know you were coming," Melvin said, physically turning Emmet back towards the residence.

"Are you having a party?" Emmet asked, but he did not sound like himself.

"Just playing some music."

"Can I meet your friends? I don't know any of your friends."

"That's okay. Maybe another time. Let's just get you back to the house."

"Do your friends know who I am?"

"Emmet, let's not bother ourselves with that."

"I love you."

"I love you too. Come on, now."

He guided Emmet all the way up the path to the residence. The musicians kept playing, seemingly in their own world.

The physical realities of my existence prevent me from knowing what transpired indoors, what words were exchanged and at what volume. Regardless, I knew this was an unexpected and potentially significant rupture in the normal proceeding of things. Did Emmet know that this was now a proper music house, no longer exclusively the site for casual gatherings among friends but rather simultaneously a money-making venture? I expected the conversations would be awkward and might involve more secrets, or their undoing.

I was left to sit with my own speculations. A nagging question was why Emmet had been in such a state of extreme inebriation. I had seen him enjoy adult beverages before. He was considered affable and was always eliciting laughter and good cheer from those around him, including during his more work-oriented discussions. They would inevitably shift into more jovial affairs, with loosened ties, loud jokes, and banter to spare. He had never ended up in such an altered state before, though, at least not here.

I did not understand all the intricate details by any means and so could not draw my own tidy conclusions about the implications of his choices, but Emmet was living a complicated life; that I knew for certain. Melvin was as well, in both similar and different ways. There were things about the world around us even all Emmet's money could not address.

The day after Emmet left, I heard a clarifying conversation between Melvin and Michio.

"Emmet's parents died," Melvin said. "Would you be able to plant something in their memory, a pair of trees or maybe a garden?"

"Oh dear," Michio replied. "I'm so sorry. Yes, of course I will. That is a thoughtful gesture."

"Thank you, Michio."

"May I ask what happened?"

"It was a car accident."

The news was shocking. The Harringtons. Louise and . . . I had never once learned Lucy's father's name. I had not learned his name and now he was gone. Lucy's parents were gone. I do not know if she felt it, but my heart reached out for her.

Michio planted two oak trees. He chose the top of a hill in a quiet section. When enough time had passed and the trees had grown mighty, their acorns would roll down.

• • •

Some time later, Melvin arrived at the pool with another man. When they moved into the music area and the man began to play the piano, the sound wrapped right around me.

The man sang, wondering whether his music would go in circles or fly like a bird. Melvin danced, his body bouncing with the exhilaration of the rhythm.

When there was silence and I was released from the dazzling embrace, I moved closer and sensed it immediately. While the song radiated jubilance, the man was cloaked in something much more complex.

"Billy, I have never once sat still for that song," Melvin said. "It is energy personified, musicalized. I have no words to express my love for what you've brought into this world."

"Oh, you've got plenty of words from what I hear."

Melvin smiled. "I'm doing my thing. It's hard . . ."

Billy nodded slowly. "I feel you."

Melvin mirrored Billy and nodded slowly too. "How do you carry it all?"

"With swagger." Billy laughed, then smiled, but even that quickly dissipated. "Nah, I don't know, I don't think I do carry it all."

"I've seen the changes—out there, I mean."

"Yeah, no doubt. But a lot doesn't change."

They sat in silence, and I held their feelings close.

"But what about you, really?" Billy asked. "You can't let them keep you caged."

Melvin sat with the words and their meaning. So did I. Somehow, I knew that as Melvin had sung many times over the years, change was coming, even here.

It took a few hundred more suns, but I felt it unfolding as if in slow motion. Melvin assembled Michio and Eliana at a table and explained that he had saved some money and was going to be moving to Minneapolis to work with a musical genius. With a smile, he said that what he would lose in sunlight, he would gain in opportunity. Melvin became choked up thanking them and saying what an honor it was to have shared this space with them. Eliana even had a tear and then shook it off, seeking to maintain her composure.

I did not know what Melvin's departure would mean for this place and those of us within it. I had been so worried about Emmet as the new proprietor, yet it turned out he was less important than those who had actually filled this space.

Eliana and Michio were vocally pleased for Melvin, but also visibly anxious. Peacock wailed in the distance.

Not long after, the group gathered around the pool and the next stage of evolution became clear. Eliana, Michio, and Ayame were going to run the place and welcome nonmusical guests as paying visitors. The days of this being a proper music house were over.

"Have y'all got a new name planned?" Melvin asked, pouring wine for everyone.

"We haven't gotten that far yet," Eliana replied. "We want to first make a few adjustments, not things that cost much money, just some reorganizing. Before we approach Emmet with a new name—and we will—we want him to see that Ayame and I have a solid handle on things."

This was an intriguing set of developments, and I was not sure how to react.

Eliana's attention drifted, and she looked to be listening. The sound of an engine, winding up the driveway.

"That is strange. Are you expecting anyone, Melvin?"

"No, ma'am. Do you want me to go and see who it is?"

"No, no. This is your last night. Please enjoy. I will go and see."

Melvin's last night. It had indeed arrived. I felt a pit in my stomach, good news about who was going to be taking over the daily management of this place notwithstanding.

When Eliana walked back towards the pool, she was not alone. Another woman was with her. An elegant woman in a dress and heels.

"Oh, sweet Jesus," Melvin said quietly.

Michio and Ayame looked at him with uncertainty. As did I.

"I think that's Emmet's wife," he said.

Awkwardness is a distinctly human feeling, experience, and energy. Tortoises and other animals have nothing comparable. At times I have enjoyed hanging out right in the center of the awkwardness, basking in its strange waves of sound and silence, the presence that everyone can feel and no one can see. Wondering how it will be banished and by whom. This, however, was not an awkwardness I relished.

Michio and Ayame stood up, but Melvin remained seated. Eliana's face was taut. She kept pace with the woman, who marched right over to the group.

"Good evening, everyone," the woman said, sitting down.

"This is Mrs. Harrington," Eliana said, remaining standing.

Mrs. Harrington looked to Ayame and Michio. "Doralee is fine."

"Hello, ma'am," they said, gently bowing. The awkwardness was circling, threatening to trap everyone within its grasp.

"So, you're the one who is going to be running this place—Ayame, is it?"

"That's right, ma'am. I will be managing along with Eliana."

"But you're the one with business experience."

Ayame looked at Eliana ever so quickly, her face stoic. "My family has a flower shop."

"Right," Doralee said. "It occurred to me that you might have studied in Japan. That's where you're from, isn't it?" Her eyes moved back and forth between Ayame and Michio.

"I'm from San Francisco, ma'am."

Doralee looked around. "It is nice here. I see the appeal. You'll get some guests." She looked everywhere but at Melvin. It was as though he were not a tortoise length away from her, sitting at the very same table. She even noticed me, watching from the shade.

"What a strange creature. Is that a giant turtle?"

Michio simply nodded. Then silence. The energy had stopped spinning. It simply hovered. No one could escape.

"It's a pleasure to make your acquaintance, ma'am, but I'm afraid we must get going. We need to pick up our daughter."

"What's her name?"

"Lily."

"And how old is she?"

"Nearly twelve."

"My daughter just turned eleven. Before you know it, she'll be driving! Goodness, I cannot bear the thought." Doralee laughed alone.

The awkwardness crackled.

"Well, maybe I'll be seeing you again. Please don't run this place into the ground." She took the wine bottle and read its label. "I'm sorry. There was no need for that sort of rudeness. My mother would be mighty ashamed of me. Please do accept my apology."

"Certainly, ma'am. There's no need to apologize," Ayame said. But, of course, there was.

"It was a pleasure to meet you," Michio said. He and Ayame glanced at Melvin and Eliana, then began to walk out, turning as though they were going to walk in the direction of the little gate.

"No, no, this way," Eliana said, gesturing towards the residence. Eliana wanted them to leave through the front despite Doralee's presence. Perhaps in spite of it.

"Y'all take care now," Doralee said as the trio walked away. She sat there looking around at the view. Melvin kept his eyes on her. She pointed at the wine and then finally looked right at him.

"Have you got anything stronger?"

Melvin walked to the bar, and Doralee studied him.

"You'd better get one for yourself too," she said.

He filled her glass, and she gestured for him to add more. He kept his serving smaller.

"Thank you," she said, swallowing a generous amount. "So, you're from the South?"

"Yes, ma'am. I'm originally from Macon, Georgia."

"Where are your parents? Are they Christians?"

"Baptists. They're still in Georgia."

"Did they know?"

"Know what, ma'am?"

"That you were . . . like this? I'm sorry, maybe I'm being a little less than polite and a bit too direct, but I don't think it's unreasonable given the circumstances."

I could not predict what Melvin was going to do. I could feel his heartbeat, though, pounding like a drum.

"My mother says she did," he simply said.

"See, now that doesn't surprise me. Women are more attuned to the details, the subtleties of people. Maybe some men see it, but they don't want to believe."

The two sat in silence. Doralee took another drink.

"I think I knew early. I sensed something. I didn't want to believe either." She held up her empty glass, indicating that she wanted more spirit to be added. Melvin poured.

"He has three kids, you know. They are unaware of all this, mercifully."

"He loves them deeply." Melvin paused. "And he loves you too."

She opened her mouth to reply but then closed it and sat in silence for some time. Melvin's face was completely neutral.

"What you need to know is that I was raised to believe y'all are a sin. But I know he was suffocating under the weight of the lies. That doesn't lessen the rage I feel, though, not one bit." She sighed. "Do other people know?"

"Which people?"

"The people he works with?"

"Absolutely not."

"Yeah, he hides it real well. Unless you know him the way I do. And I guess the way you do. The only thing I appreciate is the discretion. He risked everything. Our entire family. But I'm glad he wasn't out here shouting it off the rooftops at least."

"Do you think he had a choice?"

Doralee looked shocked. "Choice? You want to talk about choices? I wanted to go to college, you know. I'm as good with numbers as my father was. I raised it once and then never again." She took a big drink. "I couldn't even get a credit card on my own until a few years ago."

Melvin paused and looked to be considering whether to reply or not. Then he did. "I couldn't either."

"What?"

"I couldn't get a credit card either."

A hint of pink waltzed across her cheeks, and she took a big drink.

"You know, on the flight I was thinking about whether I would feel better or worse if you were a pretty girl. A blonde, redhead . . ."

Melvin shifted in his seat.

I recognized the beat before the singing started. It was undeniable.

Melvin and Doralee sat there as the harmonic voices from the radio filled in the silence. "Ah, ha, ha, ha, stayin' alive, stayin' alive."

Doralee finally spoke. "Do you love him?"

"I did."

"Meaning you don't now?"

"I do but I want something bigger."

She laughed instantly. Loudly. "Bigger than all this?" She spread her arms out.

"It's complicated. I adore it here, but I need more. My soul needs more."

"Oh, your soul!" Her voice shot right up. "I see. You put my entire family at risk, and this isn't even enough for you?" She had tears in her eyes.

"I know you're angry, Doralee. I completely understand why you are furious. But this is all extremely complicated. I was in love with him. I would have sat in some tiny apartment if that's what it took."

"But it didn't. You didn't fall for some ordinary man. You didn't sit in some dingy apartment. You lived here. Wealth beyond your wildest dreams."

"That's just the thing. Wealth isn't my dream."

A tear fell from her eye, and she quickly wiped it away. "How do you feel about all this? All of it? The deception. The secrets. The utter humiliation I feel."

"I feel a lot of things," Melvin said.

"Me too." She stood up. "What is that awful wailing sound I keep hearing?"

"The peacock."

She snorted. "The peacock. Of course there's a peacock." She started to walk away, and Melvin stood up. She stopped and turned around. "I wasn't going to come here." She straightened her dress. "I don't actually blame you. But I wanted you to have to look me in the eyes. And I want you to know that this hasn't broken me."

"I never wanted to break anyone."

Without another word, she walked back towards the residence. Melvin sat back down as the sound of the engine sliced through the air. It was not a long time by tortoise standards, but Melvin sat in silence for what still felt like a long time.

The Kindness and Cruelty of Strangers

AYAME, MICHIO, AND Lily moved into the small house behind the residence, which had been unoccupied since Mr. Williams's time. Then Eliana and Ayame physically moved around—a lot. Around the pool. Up at the residence. Back at the pool. This was all because of who was at both the pool and the residence: strangers.

Admittedly, the musicians had technically been strangers too, especially at first. But because they were guests of Melvin's, invited visitors with something very specific to learn and share, that felt different. More controlled. These were rotating strangers who varied weekly. Families with noisy children. Families with quiet children. Clusters of couples. Groups of friends. Some were tidy. Others were very messy. The latter was disconcerting, undoubtedly.

The strangers would stay at the house and eat by the pool or behind the residence, or both. They would swim and lounge in the sun and shade. They would stare at the caged birds. They would wander around. Some would sit and read. One girl proudly told her mother about the book she was reading, which was narrated by a horse. It sounded exceptional, and I desperately wished she would read aloud. Another raised a thought-provoking topic: the health of free birds beyond these walls following the banning of something I could not properly decipher. But her friend quelled the topic.

"Can you please just put down the doomsday drum for a few days? I, for one, would like to enjoy my vacation."

Both of these developments made me long for Lucy.

To make the visitors' enjoyment possible, Ayame and Eliana tended to their every need and request, whether made politely or rudely. Despite what was clearly a stressful and time-consuming project, Ayame and Michio never got angry at each other. Their bond seemed strong, particularly in comparison to what I witnessed among some, or maybe many, of the strangers. What I mean is those who had paired but not pair-bonded effectively. This prompted me to reflect on my own status as a single tortoise.

I thought it highly likely that I would enjoy the company of my own kind and that another tortoise could be as amiable as I am, or close to it. However, there was no irrefutable reason why every single tortoise should like each other. It was perfectly within reason that a tortoise might be disagreeable or morose. They could be insecure and therefore hostile towards what I have accomplished. Being with such an individual would be inferior to being the only tortoise, I determined, though this was all entirely hypothetical and speculative.

For his part, Emmet visited on very rare occasions, always when there were no guests. He hosted meetings and then would vanish. I do not think he stayed more than one night at a time, and he did not wander or swim.

Lily became my focus. She would often sit near me and tell elaborate stories that were not always linear or plotted in a conventional manner. This was no bother since I am most accepting of a range of approaches to narration.

When I returned from my egg laying that summer, I found Lily near the mimosa trees, drawing.

"I'm so glad you're here, dear Daisuke. Your timing is just about perfect."

A marvelous compliment indeed.

"I would like to paint you," she announced. She looked around and up. "We will start tomorrow!"

This was extraordinary news. My spirit swelled with a profound feeling of joy and anticipation.

Lily arrived, easel and paints in hand. "Good morning! How did you sleep?"

I had remained in place near the mimosa trees, thinking them an ideal complement to my coloring.

"In preparation for our portrait session, I wrote a poem. It's called 'Daisuke.'"

> *Daisuke is king.*
> *She rules with gentle wisdom.*
> *Daisuke is queen.*

Lily smiled. "What do you think? It's a haiku. My grandmother taught me how to write them. I don't know if you are a boy or a girl, so in my poem you are both."

The truth is, I had no words. It was one of the very (extremely) rare moments when I was rendered speechless.

Being the subject of a second artistic creation required me to showcase one among my many finely tuned skills: stillness. I stood proudly among the lush pink and green foliage and enjoyed the birds' songs. Lily narrated her work as she progressed, her eyes moving back and forth between her canvas and me. I was confident she would magnificently capture my essence as well as my graceful long neck.

"Whoa. What is that?" a little boy's voice said, out of nowhere.

"You're such a moron. It's a turtle," another boy said. I did not move my head because my top priority was being a good subject for Lily, but this one sounded older.

The younger boy appeared and studied the portrait. "That's pretty good."

"Thank you," Lily replied.

A girl and the older boy walked behind the easel too. He knocked down the canvas and rummaged through Lily's paints, tossing some onto the ground. He grabbed the paintbrush she was holding right out of her hand and turned towards me. I immediately retreated into myself.

"Don't!" Lily said.

I felt his touch.

"Go complain to Chairman Ping Pong."

All three of them walked away.

I do not know what he drew or wrote on me. I could not see the physical results. But I saw how they affected someone dear to my heart. She did not paint anymore that day. She gathered her supplies and took them away.

During the golden hour she and Michio arrived with a bucket and washed me. They exchanged only a few words.

"I still don't understand why he's allowed to stay."

"We went over this, Lily."

Then there was an extended silence. The smell of soap was strong, but I knew it was needed.

Michio took a deep breath as he rubbed me gently. "Maybe if that group asks to come back, we'll just happen to be full."

Lily nodded.

She did not return to paint the next sun. Or the sun after. But I remained. She had begun a portrait. A mighty tortoise among the vibrant pinks and greens of the mimosa trees. I held in place.

When Lily came back, she had a fresh canvas.

"I'm starting a new one. That one was good, but this version will be better. You need to look triumphant."

Once complete, she turned the painting around to show me. It was superb. Her portrait was gorgeous. I looked perfect. Her name was signed in the bottom corner with strong and clear letters.

Even as the days got cooler once again, the guests kept arriving. There was a good-sized group for Christmas who came from Wyoming. They were a hoot, very much into disco. It was nice to hear the Bee Gees again. Then another group came all the way from Manitoba in Canada! Like me, they found the winter weather of this place delightful and spent a significant amount of time outdoors.

I was napping in the sun not far from the swans in an area with nice clover when I heard a commotion near the mammals. I stirred myself right away and began to move in that direction to ensure everyone was okay.

Sharing this is painful.

Everyone was not okay. From afar I saw right away that Zedonk was unwell. She was lying down and kept rolling onto her back, not in her customary "oh, that feels good" sort of way at all. I could tell that nothing about her felt good. She would stand up, dig in the ground with her front hoof, lay back down, and roll again. Alpaca stared at her. Donkey was walking anxiously in a figure eight. Michio ran back towards the residence.

Donkey kept pacing and pacing, sweating from the stress. Zedonk had stopped trying to stand up and was simply lying on her side, her breathing labored. I kept walking in their direction with a profound sense of fear coursing through me. This seemed to be happening in slow motion, yet I could not move quickly enough.

A truck came barreling across the grounds; there was no road, but it made one. Michio and two other men jumped out and went into the enclosure. Donkey tried to block them! Poor Donkey was so worried about his friend and trying to protect her.

They created a sort of human fence that separated Donkey from Zedonk. They spoke to Donkey, seeking to calm him. They actually managed to guide him into the adjacent fenced area, along with Alpaca, and shut the gate.

Zedonk was so distressed. I felt her pain with every fiber in my body. I walked right up to the fence to try and comfort her. Zedonk wailed. It was a heartbreaking sound. I summoned all the love in my being. In her state of panic and pain, she needed to be enveloped in calmness and care.

The men spoke quietly with Michio.

I have thought about death. I have observed its results. Baby birds pushed from nests. People eating pieces of animals who had been alive. Ralph died in this place, away from view, but I still felt the loss. I have seen people mourning and know that grief is both physical and emotional. I was far from naive.

But I had never before witnessed life leave the body of another. I had not watched a thinking, feeling animal disappear, cease to exist as an individual with ideas and memories and dreams.

I do not doubt the intentions of what took place. Michio could not change the past; he could only affect what was going on in that very moment. I understand that it was an act of mercy. But watching bright eyes turn dull is a level of pain that is difficult to describe, and impossible to overstate.

Donkey and Alpaca tried to break through the gate. Michio selected a worthy location beyond the fenced enclosure at the base of a mighty tree and dug as fast as he could. I wondered if it was at all like the trees of Zedonk's homeland.

• • •

The loving arms of the forest called to me. The free animals shared comfort in their own ways. Perhaps they sensed that while I sought solitude, I did not truly want to be alone. I was once again part of a community whose members coexisted in a quiet harmony and welcomed my cadence.

There I remained, suspended in an extended state of mourning.

As the days eventually lengthened and warmed, I slowly began to feel more like myself. I gently began to think about life and possibility again. I made the acquaintance of a busy chipmunk with very attractive stripes. He had a mighty singing voice (if not a diverse range) and would "Chip! Chip! Chip!" to his heart's content. There was pride in his song; that was unequivocally clear.

I met my first opossum, a most intriguing-looking individual with a pointed nose and bold eyes who was carrying a seemingly endless number of babies right on her person! They were clinging to her back as she walked and yet seemed quite comfortable and secure in that location. We both were startled by the other, and then she registered me as an herbivore and no threat despite my formidable size, so continued on her way. I wondered when she had come here and why. And how. Under the gate? Maybe animals beyond these walls were curious or even heard good things and some crossed the threshold. I considered how often the reverse was true and residents became former residents, and what they found out there. If it was better or worse or more complicated for them and their kind.

Images of Lily began to fill my mind. I missed her. Had she been painting or writing poems? Surely she had mourned Zedonk's loss too, and I hoped her creative endeavors had been of more comfort than me.

As my strength finally returned, I knew I would be better able to support her, so embarked on the journey back to the hearth. As I arrived, it was immediately clear that something was off. There was no one at the pool. All of the furniture was changed. Gone were the rows of simple loungers, and in their place were clusters of bright yellow, pink, and blue chairs and even crisp white ones. That seemed an unstrategic choice since young strangers would inevitably spill on them. I am no businesstortoise, nor would I care to be, but why change all the furniture? I had only been gone for about a hundred suns, and this was a significant reimagining of the pool area. Had Emmet swooped in? Or had Doralee?

I heard an indelible voice. My twirling friend. She was emerging from the hi-fi! Her voice was intermingled with others in beautiful unison. But Lily was the top priority, and I set off towards the Yamadas' home.

When I arrived, it was completely quiet. I marched in the direction of the residence. As I got closer, I could see movement through the glass doors. A new proprietor? Could it be?

I walked with purpose around the fountain; gone was the hesitancy of earlier eras. With each step I surged, determined to establish whether this was, in fact, a new proprietor and to make my presence known, to learn who exactly he was and what he had in mind for this place and its many residents.

I passed the giant pots of flowers, and headed directly for the patio. The proprietor stepped outside. I stared.

At her.

It was Lucy!

Shelter

"MAGIC! I CAN'T believe it!"

I could not believe it either! Lucy was here! Lucy! Lucy! Lucy!

Lucy had become a woman. She had this mighty bearing, confident voice, and commanding presence. Of course she did. I would have expected nothing less. But seeing her was something to behold.

She rushed down the steps and kneeled, once again only a neck above me and able to look right into my eyes. Hers filled with tears.

"Magic, you haven't aged a day. You look magnificent."

I felt magnificent. My spirit was twirling and soaring!

Her presence, her very aura, completely consumed me. I had dared to imagine that she would return, but as more and more time passed, my optimism had transformed into hope and then was deliberately squeezed into a very small corner of my heart for safekeeping.

In that moment, I could feel the blood coursing through my veins. Where would we go? What would we do? We could do anything we wanted.

But Lucy looked at her wristwatch and sighed as she stood back up. "See you a little later, my beautiful friend."

I watched her walk back up the stairs and into the residence, admiring her colorful attire. I felt like I was levitating and rooted all at once. I basked in a glow even the sun could not match.

I began to process the full magnitude of what had transpired. She had gone back into the residence. She had said, "See you a little later, my beautiful friend." Was Lucy the new proprietor? Was this place to have its first lady proprietor? Of course, this was possible in theory, but it was not something I had witnessed before.

Was Lucy alone? What had she been doing? Where had she been? What did she do now that she was an adult? The possibilities were endless.

Banging emerged from the mammalian quadrant. When it stopped, I heard one of the world's preeminent songs: a girl's laugh. Lily! She was near the mammals, just on the other side of the trees. I carried the joy of Lucy's return with me as I moved. The hammering recommenced like a drumbeat. Around the bushes and trees and over the little hill I went, ready to observe who was creating these sounds, what exactly they were doing, and, most of all, to see Lily.

A woman and man were erecting a structure inside the mammals' enclosure. It had two walls and a roof, but one could enter or exit from the front or the back. I surveyed the new length of the fenced enclosure carefully. It had been expanded. And there the mammals were, at the far side, standing together. In fact, there were not one but two donkeys! Beside them, two alpacas! And Lily!

"Daisuke!"

The sound and word combined in beautiful music.

"I looked all over for you. I didn't know where you'd gone." Lily's tone was not annoyance; it was relief.

She sat down beside me, so I, too, gently dropped onto the

grass, and we watched as the last nails were hammered into the shelter. I kept looking at the mammals. Two donkeys! Two alpacas! Everyone had a friend who was just like them. And I had Lily, and Lucy, once again! What joy!

After the work crew moved off, the mammals began to meander towards the new structure, curious but cautious. They moved as a herd in unison and collectively decided that about thirty tortoise lengths away was close enough for now. Lily and I sat together in peace, listening to the birds.

Footsteps from behind caught our attention.

"Well, that looks great, doesn't it?" It was Lucy! She arrived beside Lily and me, and she was not alone.

"Hello there, young lady. You must be Lily?" Lucy asked.

"Yeah. Hi," Lily replied, waving.

"It's wonderful to officially meet you."

The girl with Lucy looked around at everyone but stayed silent. I studied her face. She did not look like Lucy. But she was with Lucy. She appeared to be about Lily's age, perhaps twelve or thirteen years young. Who was this little human?

"Would you like to introduce yourself?" Lucy asked her gently.

"I'm Robin," she said quietly, not looking at Lily.

"It's nice to meet you, Robin. This is Daisuke the tortoise."

Robin looked at me and smiled.

"Daisuke! I haven't heard that name in ages. Takeo was . . . he was your great-grandfather?" Lucy asked.

Lily nodded. "Yes, that's right. Daisuke means 'big helper.'"

"That is beautiful. I called her Magic. He thought it was a good name too."

The memory of Takeo joined my already bursting heart.

"So she is a girl?" Lily asked.

Lucy opened her mouth to respond but then paused briefly. "You know, I think I just assumed that."

The donkeys' curiosity became stronger than their caution, and they took a few more steps towards the new shelter.

"Well done, Eeyore. Brave boy," Lucy said.

"Which one is Eeyore?" Lily asked.

"The original. I got Donkers, the smaller and chubbier one, so he wouldn't be lonely. But Robin named them both."

Lily smiled. "The names are perfect, Robin. Did you name the alpacas too?"

Robin nodded.

"She chose excellent names," Lucy said encouragingly.

"Poof and Poppy," Robin said.

Lily threw her arms in the air. "Yes!"

Robin looked up and could not contain her grin. Neither could I.

The girls orbited around each other and then were united when Lily offered to show Robin her favorite places. I could not keep up with their brisk pace so instead positioned myself atop the closest hill to access the best possible vantage point of the girls' movements between twinkling gardens and constellations of trees. Lily and Robin would start their daily explorations after greeting me and finish by lying in the grass on either side of me. Although she was named after a bird, I watched Robin transform from quiet caterpillar to effusive butterfly, as though Lily's presence and thoughtfulness invited her true and hidden nature to emerge, knowing it would be safe. On the very topic of birds, one delightful decision the girls made together was to call Peacock Prince, and there was even a small naming ceremony to which I was cordially invited. He pranced around in full bloom for the duration.

"I haven't met your mom yet," Robin said as she sat on the ground, their afternoon of adventures winding down.

"She works a lot, and she goes to San Francisco sometimes. To help my grandparents."

Robin nodded.

"Your mom is really nice," Lily said.

Robin nodded again but did not immediately reply. She traced her own facial features with a blade of grass. "Lucy is . . . My mom died when I was nine."

Lily covered her mouth with her hands. "I'm so sorry. I didn't know."

"It's okay. I miss her every day," Robin said, and she rolled away from Lily and me. "Lucy doesn't try to be my mom, she is herself. She's pretty cool."

Since that initial and exceptional day, I had not seen a lot of Lucy. When I did, she would be wearing bright clothes that made her shoulders larger. I thought it was a smart look indeed, particularly combined with bangs that reminded me of Poof's poof. Intellectually, I knew her many preoccupations were a normal part of adult life. But I wanted to see her more, and more of her, to know who she had become and what she was doing—not just in the world, but for it.

I had gleaned from the girls' conversation that there were golden-hour plans for a gathering around the pool, and this held good potential. I set off in its direction and did not skirt around the edges or peer down from the adjacent hill; I marched right into the hearth. I arrived before everyone else and took a good look around.

There had been more changes made while I was gone. These were structural—technological, in fact. At the end of the pool where Melvin had hosted musical gatherings, there was even more new furniture, softer and thicker places for people to sit. Lucy and Robin arrived, then Lily did. They all greeted me, sat down, and got comfortable. Soon it became clear why. There was a screen with moving images. They began watching a story play out on the wall! It was as though I were approaching a window and peering through it to see people I had never before met, as they engaged in their lives.

Ayame appeared in dressier clothes than usual. She did not approach the group but rather gestured for Lily to come to her. Lucy noticed.

"Please, please, there's plenty of room," she called. "If you are in the mood for a comedy, join us."

Ayame approached but did not sit down. "We don't want to be a bother." She was looking right at Lily, trying to implore her to stand up with her eyes.

"Don't be silly. You are welcome, and so is Lily."

"Thank you very much, but I just got back from a long drive and am exhausted."

"Can I stay, Mom?" Lily asked.

Ayame looked back and forth between her daughter and Lucy, seemingly at a loss for words. Lucy was studying the situation. She breathed in as though preparing to speak but changed her mind.

"Only if it's really okay with Ms. Harrington," Ayame said.

"Ayame, please, call me Lucy, and yes, it really is."

"Okay, that is very kind. Lily, please come home as soon as the movie is over."

There was fruit on the side table, and Robin selected a slice, then reached towards me. I opened my mouth to partake, but she stopped and withdrew her hand.

"Is it okay to give Daisuke Magic a treat?" she asked.

"Yes, absolutely, honey. Daisuke Magic loves fruit." Lucy looked right at me. "How are you, my angel?"

It might have looked like I was still, but really, I was spinning with glee.

Robin turned back to me and extended her hand with a piece of orange. I gently removed it from her fingertips, and she beamed, watching me chew.

A voice emerged from the path to the residence. "Joan told me I'd be able to find a trio of exceptional women back here!"

A man, blazer off, tie loosened.

Lucy stopped the motion picture so proper greetings could be exchanged.

He made a beeline for Lily and bowed slightly. "You must be the famous Miss Lily. My name is Wade. It's a pleasure to meet you."

Lily's expression was a fusion of delight and embarrassment. "Hi," she said, waving.

"Glad you're here, Dad. How was it?" Robin asked.

"A few steps in the right direction. Are you settling in? Tough view, right?" He gestured to this place.

Robin nodded. "Lily has been showing me around."

"Well, that's wonderful." He was admiring the furniture and comfortable setup. "It looks great back here, wow." Then he sat down beside Lucy. "Hello, my love."

I stared at him. He looked to be a few years older than Lucy, but not significantly. This was the man Lucy deemed worthy of her heart. I found it difficult to imagine that someone could be truly worthy of her. But Lucy had chosen this particular man. I was certain that she had many suitors. Lucy was brilliant, compassionate, curious, and caring. She had clearly excelled in her career and no doubt had power and influence over important matters. What man would not want a woman that impressive?

"Hi there," he said to me, then turned his attention to the motion picture.

After the movie, the girls walked off towards the houses, and Wade put an old record on.

"With you I'm born again." I recognized the voice immediately. Melvin had called him Billy. He had been right here in this very spot at the piano.

Wade and Lucy swayed together in the moonlight, and I felt wrapped up in love's embrace. Wade looked at me and winked.

A man after my own heart.

Choices

THAT MAGICAL SUMMER, the only time I departed from the action was to lay my eggs. When the red, white, and blue decor began to appear, Lucy had a discussion with Joan, the new woman who helped at the house, about the plans. A small gathering, nothing fancy. "No fireworks, Magic. Don't you worry."

Overjoyed does not do justice for how I felt in that moment.

During the day, the girls would embark on their adventures, and I would rest, confident that we would coalesce. I admit that I became rather fixated on the motion pictures, too, for they offered a breadth and depth of insight into human life and lives. Love. Sorrow. Violence. Zany antics and laughter. People recognizing the errors of their ways and apologizing (that I had rarely witnessed in real life). Most noteworthy of all was the degree to which people moved around. From their workplaces to their homes or those of people they liked, disliked, or sought to like. To parties. To other countries. To planets other than Earth!

Many of these stories were not technically true, but they revealed truths nevertheless. Even those that were unequivocally figments of someone's imagination were instructive and illuminating, rich educational portraits. You can learn a lot about people by considering what stories they want to tell. You can speculate about their motivation and choices, or ask, if you have the opportunity to make their acquaintance.

Lucy helped bring stories to life. It took careful observation at her adult get-togethers for me to cogently piece together this important information. Lucy had become a maker of movie worlds. In fact, she was the one in charge of the very place where motion pictures were actually created. She had power over which stories were told and by whom.

"I'll green-light four high-probability hits so I can approve one with heart-changing potential, something more creative and moving," she explained to a guest while they were having drinks by the pool one evening. Math was never my fortitude, but after further reflection, I believe I understood the pragmatics of her formula. Why a moving story with heart-changing potential would not be exactly what most people wanted to see remained unclear, however.

These gatherings in combination with family nights also allowed me to gain a better understanding of Wade. His full name was Wade Reed (Lucy was still Lucy Harrington). Wade spent his time helping rivers, forests, and grasslands and, by extension, all those who live in them. He worked in courtrooms and sometimes even went to the White House. I began to feel he might be truly worthy of Lucy.

That summer was absolutely glorious, the heat and dryness notwithstanding. Lily and Robin would create cooling baths for me under the hose regularly. I hardly saw Ayame at all and hoped she was doing okay. Lily seemed happy spending as much time as possible with Robin and me, and content even when Lucy and Wade joined for movie nights. Michio kept mostly to himself, tending to the flora during the day, and relaxing near the Yamadas' home in the evenings.

Lucy would spend time reclining in the shade reading movie scripts, and I would sit near her and bask in the majesty of her presence. At times, she would chuckle or sigh or cross out whole pages. Sometimes she would look right at me and shake her head or smile, perhaps lost in thought about possibilities.

When the sun began descending earlier, I knew what was coming. I was prepared for it, mentally and emotionally. When school began, I positioned myself halfway between the large residence and the Yamadas' little home so the girls could find me more easily when they returned.

But Robin did not come to find me. Instead, I heard her voice calling from the mammalian quadrant. Something was awry. Perhaps someone! Now there were even more animals who could be in distress.

With love as my fuel, I set off to help. Ahead, Lucy emerged from the residence and ran towards Robin's voice. Then Michio passed me. I reached my top pace quickly and moved smoothly with determined efficiency. Ferocity, really.

As I crossed past the tree line onto the hill overlooking the mammalian quarter, I spotted Robin, Lucy, and Michio leaning on the fence. Just beyond them, Eeyore was forming a donkey wall that separated the humans from Donkers. Flashbacks of Eeyore pacing frantically while Zedonk thrashed around on the ground leaped into my mind. But Donkers was standing up. Her head was down but she was upright.

As I got closer, I saw movement lower down—underneath the donkeys, in fact. I had a perfect tortoise's-eye view.

There was a baby! Donkers had given birth!

This creature was a minuscule version of Donkers (and Eeyore for that matter), with the same bewitching brownish-gray coat, white nose, and enormous ears. Donkers was diligently licking her baby, who was standing upright but wobbly. They had spindly little legs and seemed to be mostly focused on their mother, a reasonable state of being for one who had only just joined us and knew nothing of this world.

I walked right up and stood beside the humans for the best possible view of this extraordinary development.

"I noticed she was a bit anxious yesterday, but not in an alarming way," Michio said.

"She gave birth in the shelter, I think." Robin pointed.

"I can't believe this happened," Lucy said, shaking her head.

"You weren't told she was pregnant?" Michio asked.

"I was not. I'm guessing they kept that little detail quiet on purpose. Or maybe they didn't know either. She was chubbier than Eeyore, that was obvious. But I thought she had just been eating a richer diet. God, she seems young to be a mother, but what do I know."

"Eeyore isn't the father?" Robin asked.

"No, honey. I'm sure donkeys gestate for longer than a couple of months. Plus, Eeyore isn't exactly equipped for fathering. She must have been pregnant before we got her."

"Should the vet come?"

"That's a good question. Nothing looks wrong or out of place to me. What do you think, Michio?"

"I think the baby looks normal and healthy, and Donkers too, but I'm far from an expert."

"I can't believe this!" Robin said. "Is it a girl or boy?"

Lucy studied the baby and so did Michio.

"Female, I think," Lucy said.

Michio nodded. "I think so too."

"What do we call young female horses?" Lucy asked Robin.

Robin twisted her mouth. "Foal? I'm trying to remember. This was in *The Black Stallion* ... No, wait, *foal* is for either. What is the name for females? Is it the same for horses and donkeys?"

"I believe it is."

"Filly! She's a filly."

The filly was still focused on her mother, all four legs spread out wider than would seem normal, a balancing strategy that, so far, was working well. It looked like a breeze could blow her over, though.

Robin was positively chuffed. "She's a miracle! Maybe we can call her Miracle? Mira!"

"I think you'd better wait and decide with Lily," Lucy said, and Robin nodded.

Michio smiled with his whole body.

As you have surely anticipated, I did not leave the new family's side. Mira, as she was ceremoniously dubbed later that day, managed to drink (often), stand with her legs squarely under her, walk, and even trot very quickly in a little circle around her mother. She was a marvel of development, and I was mesmerized by every chapter in this new tale, how she grew each day that passed.

The girls were overflowing with curiosity but gave the donkeys space, a decision both respectful and appropriate. Eeyore seemed to relish his new role as honorary uncle and stayed close by but without crowding Donkers and Mira. Poof and Poppy were curious but not pushy.

"Donkers seems protective," Lily said.

"That comes with the territory," Lucy said.

"I like how Daisuke Magic is keeping watch too."

They all looked at me. I was beaming with pride.

"She's seen a thing or two in her day," Lucy said.

Robin studied me. "Have you ever given birth?"

"Tortoises are reptiles, sweetheart," Lucy said, a correction, but one made gently.

"Right."

"I think they lay eggs," Lily said. "Is that right?"

There was silence. Everyone was considering this information. For his part, Eeyore took a break from his uncle duties for a roll in the dust.

"Does she lay eggs?" Robin asked. She turned to me. "Do you lay eggs?"

"She must," replied Lucy.

"But they don't hatch."

Lucy shook her head.

"There would need to be a male, right?" Lily asked tentatively. "For the eggs to hatch."

Lucy nodded. "That's right."

"What about the swans?" Lily wondered.

"I think they would be parents by now if that were going to happen."

"Are they both female?"

"I'm not sure, honey."

Lucy stepped back and put her hand on her stomach.

"Are you going to throw up again?" Robin asked.

Lucy responded with her other hand, gesturing "Wait." She stood for a second and breathed in deeply. "I'm okay."

"How old is Daisuke Magic?" Robin asked.

"Honestly, I don't know. I've never known this place without her."

Robin turned to me. "I'm glad you're still here. Is it weird to make eggs that are supposed to be babies that don't become babies?"

"Well, I wouldn't say 'supposed to be babies,'" Lucy said. "They're just eggs. They *could* become babies."

"Do you think Daisuke Magic wants to be a mother?" Lily asked.

"I couldn't say, sweetie. Being a mother is a big job. I think she has a lot going on without a baby tortoise running around at top speed." Lucy winked.

I would need time to process this discussion. Thankfully, one thing I never lack is time.

All remained well among the mammals, so I was able to watch them and think simultaneously. I pondered the intricacies and implications of that conversation for a number of suns. This was not the first time I had considered the topic of motherhood and my own motherhood, in particular. But, to my knowledge, it was the first time anyone else had.

As I have explained before, tortoise company would be lovely, provided that the individual was pleasant and ideally jovial. My interest in another tortoise was not about procreation, however; it was about companionship. There were times when I wanted a partner who moved at my pace, enjoyed similar foods and music, and relished naps. Someone who experienced the world as I did. Yet I also knew that any tortoise who came here would have a very different tale from mine, with distinct characters and experiences. Would she or he feel the same way about this place? Be interested in observing and supporting the many residents? Listening to the varied conversations? Watching movies? There was no way for me to know.

I also would enjoy teaching someone, but being a mentor, an uplifter, a guide, a muse, these roles are not synonymous with being a mother. I could be a cool auntie or a benevolent friend or simply a caring teacher, like the one who had taught me so much. No, a mother was not something I wished to be.

This was a good thing, since I had no say in the matter.

Over the next few suns, Eeyore, Poof, and Poppy remained

close to the new mom and baby but became less fixated and more relaxed about the situation. Donkers was proud of her filly and allowed each of the others to not only approach but also smell Mira. In response to their interest and gentle touch, Mira would mouth as though she was chewing the air. It was adorable indeed. I believe she was saying, "Hello, I am baby, and it is a pleasure to make your acquaintance."

Our new resident was enthusiastically welcomed into the herd, which began to resume more normal comings and goings, grazings, and nappings. Michio started to bring additional forage, which came in cubed bundles. The grass was surviving but the heat and dryness were testing its resilience, so this supplementary culinary offering seemed designed to ensure Donkers was getting enough nutrition since she was now physically responsible for feeding two. I found it intriguing that mammals carry their offspring within their bodies and then produce food specifically designed for them. I thought it odd that Lucy and Emmet had been given the milk of another animal to drink as youngsters. I wondered what had happened to the baby of the mother whose body had produced the milk being drunk by human children. I far preferred what was going on right in front of me—a baby drinking from her own mother and no one else's.

Some suns later as I dozed in and out, I heard the distinct sound of human voices drifting through the air from near the swans' pond. I proceeded through the tree line and spotted Lucy, Wade, and Robin approaching chairs that had been placed there. It was a nice spot in which to relax and observe, undoubtedly, but Lucy was wrapped up in a blanket and did not look quite like herself.

"Are you comfortable? How is the pain?" Wade asked her. Robin studied her carefully as he spoke, and Lucy sat down gingerly.

"It's getting better."

"What happened, Lucy?" Robin asked.

"Well, that's why we wanted to sit out here together—so we could talk as a family."

Robin instantly started breathing rapidly. "No, no, no. This is not happening. What was that appointment about?" It was like she had been pushed, or fallen, though she did not leave the chair.

Wade reached over and took her hand. "My angel, Lucy is not sick. Breathe, please. Breathe."

"Sweetheart, it's okay. Everything is okay," Lucy said. She tried to reach for Robin but flinched and had to sit back.

Robin consciously slowed her breathing as she stared out into the pond. I kept my distance, listening and watching but not wanting to interrupt.

"Are you okay?" Lucy asked. Robin nodded.

"Yeah. I'm sorry. I didn't mean to . . ."

"You don't need to apologize," Wade said.

"Never be sorry for feeling deeply and caring about others," Lucy said. Her eyes filled with tears. "We have so much love in our family. I think it's the perfect size as is."

Wade reached out and held Lucy's hand too. Robin looked back to the swans.

"I love you, Lucy," she said.

I understood. And felt it all.

Visitors

MIRA CONTINUED TO grow and thrive. She was unsure about the man who came to file the donkeys' hooves but tolerated his presence and tugged at his shirt with her mouth, which seemed playful, not vindictive, to me (and to him—he simply pushed Mira back gently with a hint of a smile). The foot-tending man also began trimming the alpacas' nails! That was a bit of an ordeal and required assistance from Michio. Neither Poof nor Poppy seemed to understand that the activity was designed to help them. Michio mustered significant calm and reassurance, and ultimately their toes were in tip-top shape.

"You ever had any foot issues with that?" the foot-tending man asked Michio, pointing to me.

That? Goodness gracious.

I looked at my front feet. They looked perfect.

"Not a thing. You know, I've been working here for fifteen years now and there has never been a vet or anything like that even once for the tortoise."

Michio's comments prompted me to reflect further. My feet did not require regular maintenance. But they are attached to a robust and elaborate body. What would happen if something unfortunate were to occur? An accident or injury, a sickness or, goddess forbid, an assault. Was there someone qualified to provide the appropriate care for me? Would the doctor who saw to the mammals be capable of assisting me, or were the differences between our kinds too great? Surely there would have to be suitable medical personnel to oversee tortoise health. Somewhere. Where?

I had never before considered this matter.

Did anyone else worry about this?

I was healthy. Remarkably so. I had not been unwell physically at any point. I felt occasional fatigue, but that was not surprising given the extensive journeys I took, and this sensation was temporary, easily remedied through slumber. I had experienced minor scrapes and scratches, and being submerged in the pool was damaging for many reasons, including the physical. But nothing significant had ailed me or caused lasting bodily harm.

Maybe this was why no one was concerned. My indefatigable nature. I was always here, in the expansive present, as it stretched onwards. I brought comfort; I did not cause stress.

I found this reassuring and persuasive argumentation.

As the days got cooler and Mira even larger and healthier, I set off for the hearth in anticipation of the festivities.

When I approached the pool area, there were already celebrations underway. The place was positively glowing with lights and candles. People of all ages were talking, eating, and laughing.

Lucy was commenting on the president who had previously been in motion pictures.

"That chimpanzee movie was disturbing, in retrospect," an older woman said.

I had instantly become fond of her due to her exquisite, full-bodied laugh, but showing concern for a chimpanzee made me like her even more. Wade called her nimaamaa, and Robin used nookomis, which I learned were Anishinaabemowin words for *my mother* and *my grandmother*. I had not heard this language before and was pleased to be expanding my education and understanding.

"Which movie was that, nookomis?" Robin asked.

"*Bedtime for* . . . Bongo, was it?"

"*Bonzo*," replied Lucy.

"Bonzo!" one of the teenage boys said, laughing.

Robin rolled her eyes ever so slightly. "What happened to him?"

"Well, he's in the White House."

"No, I mean the chimpanzee."

"I'm not sure." Lucy looked pensive. "That's a troubling thought. I've heard there is a woman who bought land out in the redwoods near San Francisco, where she retired all her performing tigers and cougars. Let's hope the chimpanzee went somewhere like that, without the tigers, of course." Lucy looked at me. "Daisuke Magic has given me a prehistoric idea, though. The animal on-screen would be created by computers."

"Cool!" Robin said. Cool, indeed, though I felt warmed by the fact that I continued to be a muse.

"What are the roots of the name Daisuke?" Nookomis asked.

"It's Japanese and was chosen by my best friend's great-grandfather. It means 'big helper.'"

"And she is one," Lucy replied. "A very special friend."

"She has been here a long time," Nookomis said.

Robin nodded. "That's a good point. When was she brought here?"

Everyone looked at Lucy, me included.

"Well, I don't actually know. She was here when I first arrived."

"How long ago was that?" Robin asked.

Lucy paused. "Summer of 1957."

"Whoa!" Robin stared at me. "Maybe you should try to find out for sure when she came here."

Nookomis reached her hand out towards Robin. "Can you help me up, noozis? Let's go for a little walk."

While the rest of the guests resumed other conversations and refilled their plates and cups, Robin and Nookomis walked at a tortoise's pace, and I followed.

Although I heard every word, it is not my story to tell. What I feel comfortable sharing is that Nookomis spoke of a time when people were fighting and showing disrespect for one another and the animals. Most were killed by a massive flood, though some survived by floating on a log. The remaining people and animals wanted to re-create land by collecting soil from deep under the water. Many of them drowned while trying to swim to the very bottom, including a muskrat. But within the muskrat's paw, there was a handful of soil. He had given his life, but succeeded. The people and animals spread that soil and danced together to create Earth. On the back of a turtle.

"I don't know where she comes from, and my heart says she was taken from her lands and relatives. But in another way, she has always been here. I will call her Zaagi'."

Robin's eyes were glimmering with tears. "What does that mean, nookomis?"

"It means 'love.' And 'treasure.'"

A Trick of the Tale

AS THE DAYS got longer, my excitement for the return of summer grew. Even the heat was more manageable because of the frequent hosings Robin and Lily would provide.

But my dreams for our summer together came crashing to a halt. The entire Yamada family was moving. They were going to San Francisco to care for Ayame's parents.

The girls sat together and made plans to talk on the phone and write letters. Although they tried not to, they cried. I stood near them, trying to will my love to wrap around their hearts. I rocked back and forth on my legs, buzzing from the pain.

I saw the boxes being removed from the Yamadas' home and dragged myself closer to say farewell to Michio and Ayame too. Once they were gone, that area felt like a cave. I moved towards the residence, hoping to catch a glimpse of Robin or Lucy or even dear Wade, but it was alarmingly quiet. After many suns of waiting in vain, I felt compelled to reconnect with someone, anyone.

I returned to the mammalian section and mercifully my furry family members seemed well. Yet as I walked to the swans' home, something felt different. There were a few frogs. But the swans were gone.

I climbed back up the hill to the residence and placed myself right by the fountain, prepared to stay indefinitely. Time became something of a blur, so I cannot say how long I was there.

Finally, I heard sound from within the residence, and my heart whizzed with excitement. Through the glass doors I saw Joan, whose presence was consistently calm and caring. The mere sight of her brought me comfort in this moment. She noticed me, too, and descended the steps with a piece of apple. I was grateful for her generosity, though the fruit did not taste as sweet.

The sound of vehicular doors being closed on the far side of the residence was the first suggestion that some normalcy might resume. Lucy came out and kneeled so she was but a neck's length taller than me once again.

"You are such a devoted friend," she said, rubbing my neck.

I wanted to say thank you and that it was easy to be a devoted friend to those who are truly worthy. I wished I could ask about the swans and how Robin was doing. Who would be moving in to fill the small house and would they have a new friend, a child who would love flowers and bees and poetry?

Instead, I waited quietly, as I always do. Lucy sat with me, on the ground, in her fancy outfit. I do not know how long we remained together like that, but I can tell you it felt like her heart was my own.

When Robin finally emerged, she saw me but did not approach. Instead, she went off towards the pool with a book. I marched in her direction, but by the time I arrived, she was gone.

Unfortunately, this pattern continued. She eventually began

saying hello, but instead of seeking comfort in my company, it was as though my very presence made her feel sadness, perhaps a reminder of her time with Lily. This realization was a deep wound. I placed myself in the learning pod and remained suspended in melancholy.

The sound of girls' voices eventually stirred me both literally and figuratively. Robin appeared in front of me with a girl who seemed familiar, even though I had never seen her before.

"This is Magic," Robin said.

The girl's mouth opened as she looked at me. I stared right back, studying her face. She almost looked like a young Lucy. But that was not quite right.

"Your dad and I spent a lot of time right in this area when we were kids, Aspen," Lucy said, appearing and putting her arms around both girls. "That was a very special time, wasn't it, Magic?"

Lucy was certainly correct that our earliest time together had been magical.

The features. Her dad . . .

Was this . . . ?

This was Emmet's daughter!

"Hi, Magic," she said.

"Magic is a tortoise," Robin said, looking at me, not Aspen. Her voice sounded quieter, more like it had when she had first arrived, as though she had tucked back inside herself.

"Where is Magic from?" Aspen asked.

Both girls looked at Lucy, who sighed. "You know, I need to find out. I don't exactly know how I'm going to do that, but I will see what I can do."

A flurry of energy surged through my body. This proposition was thoroughly enlivening. Lucy was finally going to apply her dazzling mind in search of my homeland. This elusive and almost ethereal place that existed in my sensory memories would become real.

For their part, the two girls began to explore the grounds together, but this time it was Robin serving as tour guide and teacher, and she excelled in these roles. The full version of Robin slowly peeked out and then stepped gingerly into the light. Aspen was nothing like her father when he was a boy, or an adult for that matter. She was distinctly her own person; if anything, she was more like Lucy: attentive, gentle, introspective, I dare say. Prince found her most worthy of an extended plumage display, much to Aspen's delight. Robin and Aspen would happily hang out together near the pool or in the gardens or by the mammals with me at their side. For seven suns, the energy of girls shone as brightly as the sun once again, filling this place with quiet joy.

But then Aspen was gone and Robin seemed to retreat back into herself. Until something suddenly changed. She began to run. She ran short sprints or more slowly for longer periods of time. I did not even try to keep up or follow, but instead watched as she traversed every inch of this place as I had done in my earliest time here, albeit at a much more appropriate pace.

This running continued as the days became cooler. Upon return from school, she would run each and every golden hour. One evening, as she passed by the learning pod where I had positioned myself, she was not alone. There was a four-legged yellow being running at Robin's side! A dog!

"Hang on a minute there, young lady," Lucy called from the lounger nearby where she was reading a script. "What is going on? Who is this?"

Robin and the golden sphinxlike creature slowed, then stopped. The dog sat down and looked at Lucy, her pointy ears on full display.

"This is my new friend. She's been hanging around the gate."

"By the gate out front," Lucy said, more statement than question.

Robin nodded. "Yeah, well, until now. I think she'd like to stay. I'd like her to stay."

I shifted in place, and in that moment, the dog noticed me. She walked right up to me and stopped about a tortoise length away. She tilted her head to the side. I moved my leg again, and she made a muffled sort of grumbling sound but then approached. She extended her long nose towards me and we booped. She pulled her head back but then reapproached—and licked me!

Lucy laughed. "Oh, for goodness' sake. Did you plan this?"

Robin shrugged, but her smile beamed. "Can we name her Sunbeam?"

"I think that's just about perfect."

Sunbeam had physical scars on her face yet was a most amiable individual. I wondered what had happened to her before, but knew she had made an outstanding choice by selecting this place's gate and this girl. Sunbeam refrained from chasing Prince after an entertaining initial encounter I had the pleasure of observing directly. Notably, Sunbeam was given a special status as both animal resident and human companion. She went inside the residence with Robin.

Sunbeam and Robin were always together. They moved around much too quickly for my liking, but it seemed the ideal pace for Sunbeam. Through the wonderful holiday celebrations, which again burst with love and light, and even occasional visits from other girls who were quite pleasant, Robin and Sunbeam were inseparable.

The following summer, Aspen returned—and stayed for longer. Her arrival did not slow the Robin-Sunbeam extravaganzas. Aspen did not run, and preferred to read, or sit with Lucy near the pool and talk or listen to music during the day. At night, Robin and Aspen would dance by the pool or lie around looking at the stars. Aspen knew the names of the constellations, but they would also make up new names. Seahorse. Fanny Pack. Magic Land (that made me twinkle).

In previous years, Robin's birthday had been celebrated with smaller family dinners by the pool, but something larger was being planned. Robin was turning fourteen! She was strong and getting taller. I saw her growing right before my eyes.

The pool was the center of the festivities, and I opted to place myself right in the heart of the action near the water, despite the painful memory of what happened to me at a party of a similar size when Lucy was but a few years older than Robin. I recognized the girls from the occasional visits, and they had shown me no malice, so I felt comfortable among this crowd and confident that my personal safety was not in danger. The girls played games, lounged by the pool reading magazines, and either sat on its edge or jumped right in. Lucy, Wade, and a couple of other adults drank cocktails in the shade. Prince made a dramatic entrance once he heard the commotion, flipping his tail fan open to its full majesty as he entered the vicinity, causing quite a scene. He paraded right through center stage, and many of the girls clamored to stand behind him as Wade took photos.

"Prince, you're on the radio!" Robin announced. It was a very catchy song about a car and horses. Something about it reminded me of Melvin, not the lyrics, but the music, its energy and zest, really.

Prince (the person, not the peacock!) sang about finding a love that would last. I wondered if Melvin had. I hoped he had.

The pool jumping generated splashes that were a welcome antidote to the intensity of the heat. One of the girls apologized to me after she realized her cannonball had sent water in my direction, unaware that it was most appreciated, though I also respected her manners. Another of the girls ran over to the stereo and turned up a song that brought great excitement. It was a blast from the past, and more memories of Melvin rushed back, albeit for a very different reason.

"Ah, ha, ha, ha, stayin' alive, stayin' alive."

A number of the girls had an entire choreographed dance routine to accompany it. Sunbeam ran over and created some beautiful chaos, then Wade tried to show off his moves, and Robin pushed him away, mortified. He shrugged for the other parents, who applauded and laughed.

As the sun began its descent, Joan arrived wheeling a massive cake and everyone cheered. Lucy assisted with the distribution of slices and Wade continued to take photos.

"May I be in the picture with the tortoise, Mr. Reed?" one girl asked.

"Of course! But be quick, she might take off."

Hilarious, Wade. Hilarious.

The girl waved Robin over, and the two of them kneeled on either side of me. They both smiled, their thumbs in the air. Then they flitted off towards the cake and I wondered whether Joan had brought any fruit down.

"Do you want some cake, Debbie?" Robin asked a girl who was sitting nearby stretched out on a lounger.

"No, thanks. I am trying to avoid looking like that," and she pointed at me.

At me! To what was she alluding? How would cake make her look like me?

She puffed out her cheeks and used her hand to trace an imaginary belly well in front of where her actual stomach was located.

I was utterly aghast. She was mocking my form. I am a superb shape and can think of no better shape for me to be.

"You're fine, though," this Debbie said. "You're basically a rake. Can I have some apple?"

Ever-generous Joan had indeed brought a slice of fruit down, correctly anticipating my presence and thoughtfully preparing accordingly so that I could partake in the culinary cheer too. She handed the apple slice to the girl.

"Say cheese!" Wade said, and the girls all presented their teeth for the camera.

My prediction about not being in physical danger around teenage girls was proved correct. I had no idea it was my heart that would be hurt.

I had never before seen a girl turn into a full-blown teenager, but it unfolded right before my eyes. Robin never became certifiably rude but would be cranky with Lucy and Wade sometimes. It was peculiar to watch. Their reactions varied depending on the situation or moment in time, sometimes seeming thoroughly displeased and in other instances more resigned to their fate. Or this phase. Whatever it was.

Robin continued to run with Sunbeam and added swimming to the mix. She would power her way through the water, a far cry from the usual sort of bobbing and floating that took place. Robin would still pause to say hello and offer me fruit when our paths crossed from time to time. I could not help but wonder if she would have wanted to spend more time with me if I were able to move more quickly.

Aspen visited each summer. She would read and write and seemed comfortable spending a lot of time in her own mind with my supportive presence at her side. I wondered about her father and mother, both where they were and how they were.

On some occasions Aspen, unfortunately, employed the technology of the Walkman (Walkwoman?) to enjoy music in plain sight but without anyone hearing the sound but her. At other times, she would listen on a small and movable stereo, which was clearly a convenient option for portability despite the decline in sound quality. I still appreciated its use because of the dynamic music of the era. There really was quite a range. Much of it was catchy and energizing, but some of it was darker. Aspen would always turn an especially evocative song called "Meat Is Murder" up to a high volume. It was a powerful sensory experience and even included the sounds of cows. I found it very affecting.

One evening, it was only Wade and Lucy alone together beside the pool. He was updating her about a lawsuit involving a forest. I must have nodded off, not out of a lack of interest but rather due to the intense heat of the day, because the next thing I heard was Wade's voice at augmented volume: "You hear that, Magic? Our beloved Lucy has unlocked the secret of your identity. You are a giant tortoise. I, for one, am shocked!" He laughed.

"Wade, stop. It's something."

"I'm just teasing you, my love. Of course it is. Let's toast to Magic." He raised his glass in the air.

A giant tortoise.

Giant. How exquisite.

This must mean there were smaller tortoises. Medium-sized tortoises. Was size a significant matter in tortoise society? Tortoise societies? Did we cohabitate or live in distinct clusters with like-sized individuals? Were we all categorized by size, or were there other measures and groupings?

I had many unanswered questions, but Lucy was right: It was something. I had tempered my initial excitement about her obtaining valuable information about my origins when I heard nothing further. In fact, I had deliberately suppressed thoughts of the possibility and been practicing what I had heard people describe as "living in the moment." But Lucy had not forgotten! Despite all her responsibilities and demands, how very busy she was, she had kept her word and searched for clues to my mystery, to our mystery.

She would keep searching. I felt certain she would.

I watched Lucy closely during this era whenever she was around because I was intrigued by how she was navigating this significant period of change in Robin. I was experiencing something similar, as Mira grew into a feisty young donkey with a spark-filled personality and seemingly boundless energy. She was nearly as tall as her mother, and would alternate between staying close to her herd and wandering off on her own, for her own reasons. Nevertheless, it was clear that Mira was far more straightforward than a teenage girl, a particularly mercurial kind of being.

The biggest change happened both quickly and at a tortoise's pace somehow—Robin became a woman. One fall, she departed for her educational endeavors and did not return in the evenings at all. She went to university on the other side of the country. Sunbeam stayed behind and spent a lot of time with Joan in particular, since she was here the most. I would watch Joan walk with Sunbeam, and it was nice to see her being able to actually enjoy this place and all its beauty.

Lucy hosted more parties for people from the motion pictures, some very proper and others most animated and replete with debauchery. I would often participate and found I was able to be something of a night owl when the spirit moved me. The magnificent repertoire of Phil Collins permeated throughout many of these gatherings, which was one of my favorite parts. Truly, I cannot imagine my life without his voice. I also delighted in the chic and colorful fashions of this era, the giant shoulders rivaled only by the enormity of the hairstyles.

I even became included in the ground rules. Lucy would get everyone's attention, welcome them, provide some requisite pleasantries, and then: "We have only three rules. First, no glass near the pool. Second, no pajamas!" Everyone would laugh at the latter. At one party, a man in the crowd yelled back in a most serious tone, "I am personally offended by this assault on my character and fashion!" But my worry promptly subsided when people started laughing, including the man himself.

Lucy always saved the most important rule for last: "Third, do not bother the tortoise." It would invariably result in more laughter from the crowd for reasons unbeknownst to me but, crucially, was respected.

Lucy would thank some people in the crowd for "tremendous work" or "visionary creativity" or "heartrending rawness." She singled out a Mr. Williams for "a unique generosity of spirit that fills our souls with hopeful joy." I became animated at the prospect of this being *the* Mr. Williams, the very teacher who had taken my mind to new heights, but it was a different person. This Mr. Williams had people in stitches during the party (some laughed so hard they had to wipe happy tears from their cheeks) but then lingered quietly afterwards, sitting by the pool alone. He smiled at me. "Hello, friend," he said, and we remained side by side in a state of gentle communion. He was buoyant, but sadness hovered within him too.

As he left, Lucy hugged him. "You wouldn't believe the stories this one has told me," he said. "My, what this humble not-so-little tortoise has seen." Our time together was brief, but I kept some of his tender heart with me.

Various less-wonderful people at these parties would speak to me. On one occasion an item was placed on my back (which was swiftly removed by a helpful bystander, a noble person clearly familiar with the ground rules and basic matter of respect). Someone tripped over me during a particularly raucous evening but caused me no harm, and I believe it was genuinely an accident.

"I would love to read lines with you."

"Only my agent talks more than you."

"E.T. phone hooome."

Oh, how they found their comments endlessly comical.

There was another man who was inarguably funny, however. He had this frenetic energy surging through him and seemed to be operating more quickly than everyone else yet was somehow also calm. It was a delightful combination.

"I loved you in *Baby*," he said upon first encountering me. "You, Catherine, Andrea, and Eugene—now that would be a picture worth seeing."

Later: "That's the thing about auditioning in Canada." He had the entire party's attention. "You go in, you nail it, they say you're good, and you get to talking, everyone the very epitome of politeness. At some point, the producer apologizes for needing to get going, so you say no, no, I'm sorry, and it just turns into this neverending loop of sorrys, and the next person's audition is late, so you step into that hallway and apologize to everyone waiting."

A white-haired man piped in and said, "Ladies and gentlemen, this is why Hollywood is in LA, not Toronto." So much laughter.

As the party was winding down, the frenetic man remained and asked Lucy's permission to play a record.

"You just carry records with you to parties?" she asked.

"You know, sometimes I like to give them out as gifts, even when I'm not the host. It's just a nice touch. 'Here, have a party favor.'" She laughed and shook her head with a smile. "Ms. Lucy—may I call you Ms. Lucy? I have the perfect soundtrack. I am representing a bit here. Supporting my own, if you will. Someone's got to!"

He put on the record, and I immediately enjoyed the sound.

"That's catchy as hell, Marty," another guest said.

Wade was nearby, and he nodded. "Great production."

"The Slugs," Marty said.

"Sorry?"

"This is the magical sound of Doug and the Slugs. Marketing experts they were not!"

"Day by day," Doug sang. I felt moved. It was like a theme song, something that captured my essence. Was this how I approached life? Was I becoming stronger, not only physically but also emotionally? I was. Which was crucial preparation.

Time Is Relative

SUNBEAM'S FACE AND even her eyelashes became gray. She and Joan moved more slowly, and sometimes I would walk at their side, because I was able to keep up.

One day, Robin appeared and joined them as they strolled in a flat grassy area. Tears streamed down her face, and she kept stopping to hug Sunbeam. Somehow, even without the words being uttered, I understood why. I moved myself as close as I could to the residence, and everyone saw me waiting. Sunbeam stopped and licked my face. Robin was soaked in tears.

As the sun began to set, they buried Sunbeam under the soil near a rich yellow garden. I would visit it and honor Sunbeam, a remarkable survivor who found the strength to forgive and love those who were truly worthy.

It was quite some time before I saw Robin again. I found her harder to read. She seemed well but also serious, as though worry was coursing through her. Based on a conversation I overheard about this very topic, I learned that this tension was part of becoming an adult. I realized I had long felt the same from Lucy. She was the same person, but had to be different too. Everyone was aging. Mira had become a grown-up donkey, and she was hearty and hardy, while Poof's and Eeyore's movements slowed. That is what happens with time.

Time meant Robin created a life beyond this place. She would always return home for the winter holiday season, which continued to be vibrant, although the number of older people who attended dwindled, and some people whom I would not previously have described as older began to look that way. Aspen would come by sometimes, and she began joining for part of the festive season. I wondered whether Emmet would reappear too, but he did not, and I overheard no discussion of him and his whereabouts, or Aspen's mother for that matter.

Lucy and Wade went to Spain to watch Robin run in the Olympics! She was that fast! I cheered Robin on from afar. I felt proud that this place had helped her become so strong. I had thought she was running away, but she was running towards. Or maybe it was both.

That summer, I realized I had neither heard nor seen Prince in quite some time, and was forced to accept what that meant. I hoped his end was peaceful and not painful, and that he had found joy here, even though he was the only one of his kind and this was not his homeland either. Truthfully, I was unsure when it happened. Even in the days when he was preoccupied with impressing poolside guests, Prince would spend periods of time alone in the far reaches of this place. Nevertheless, I felt ashamed that I could not identify how long it had been since I had heard him, let alone seen him. His wail had become part of the soundtrack of this place.

I retreated to the forest sanctuary to ponder these significant changes, the departures and especially the losses. What remained consistent was me. I had been here before every one of the current residents. My existence seemed to stretch out for an unknowable amount of time. Why was I here for so long while others were not? Was this fair? Was this desirable? Was I grateful for this time, for this great expanse of time? Seeing, hearing, witnessing, and being part of so much and the lives of so many was simultaneously awe-inspiring and unsettling.

As the holiday season arrived, I was worried about who would not be there.

The reverse turned out to be the risk.

Robin had brought young men home on occasion, but that year, the one with her was quite a hit. His name was Easton.

"Easton, this is a special friend, Magic," Robin said when he first stood near me.

He looked down, (rudely) said "Ha ha, weird," then moved on. Robin rubbed my neck and continued onwards with Easton.

He was very outgoing, and people seemed to enjoy his antics over the following days. I remained unconvinced.

Some time later, a party was held around the pool to celebrate his engagement to Robin. I observed and continued to be uncertain. I tried to be celebratory like everyone else, but Easton took up so much space and air, it bothered me. He bothered me.

Later there was an epic fiesta around the pool comprised entirely of women, so it reminded me of the parties Aspen and Robin had held when they were teenagers. I wondered if any of those same girls were in attendance, and whether it mattered. If those had been real friends or not. Robin had become a different and stronger person, perhaps more than what some people could appreciate.

As each guest arrived, I cautiously hoped Lily would be among them. Sadly, she was not. Surely Lily and Robin had stayed connected to each other at least initially, as they had so fervently planned to do, despite the geographic distance. What had happened to end their friendship? An eruption or simply a slow drift, the passage of time compounded by the distance?

The party was a raucous occasion. I stayed in the vicinity to enjoy the large quantity of Shania Twain's music that was being played, songs of the highest lyrical and instrumental quality.

The wedding involved extensive planning and preparation, and for a brief, fleeting moment, I was reminded of the traveling symphony. But I forced myself not to dwell in the past but rather to focus on the future. Robin had decided to marry this man, and I would support her despite my concerns. Leon, the new garden artist, worked overtime to ensure the flowers were their most beautiful. Lucy placed a robust and colorful garland around me for the occasion. No doubt I looked radiant.

As the guests arrived, I noticed someone familiar immediately. It was Emmet, his hair still full but gray. He was with another man, and both of them hugged Lucy and shook hands with Wade enthusiastically. Emmet seemed happy, I think. I wondered whether he would walk around the gardens and show his companion the majesty of this place, what had once been his home too. But Emmet remained focused on the ceremony. Aspen stood at Robin's side and wiped away a tear. Afterwards, there was music and dancing. Robin gave a lovely speech and so did Aspen. Easton delivered a long speech that was more about him than Robin. When Robin danced with her father, I did not let my mind linger on how different Wade was from Easton.

Later a celebration of the impending baby birth was held. More than one joke was made about Robin's belly looking like me. That was not inaccurate, and I took it as a compliment. Admittedly, I did stare at Robin's significantly expanded stomach area, within which the future human was growing, this peculiar mammalian practice. *Distinct*, that is a better word.

"Have you settled on name possibilities?" one of Robin's friends asked her.

"Probably Jasmine if it's a girl, and Easton really likes Dylan for a boy," Robin replied. "I'm not a big fan of Dylan because I just picture Bob Dylan or *90210*, but Easton really likes it."

"What boys' names do you like?"

"Oh, Dylan is the winner, I think. Easton is pretty insistent. I think he's hoping for a boy."

It was Jasmine who arrived with Robin the next visit, a minuscule human who was basically the size of my head and neck.

"Jasmine, these are your grandparents," Robin said. Lucy's eyes filled with tears.

Lucy was a grandmother. It hardly seemed possible. Although she was mighty, I knew this fact was indicative of Lucy's advancing age. It was a topic I deliberately and consistently avoided. In this instance, I refocused my thoughts on Jasmine. She blew bubbles and had quite a powerful set of lungs. I wondered if she was going to be a singer. I could be her muse and wanted her to learn of my impeccable credentials.

Robin and Jasmine visited more often, and both grandparents enjoyed fawning over the new addition. But Robin seemed different. I do not mean different from the teenage version of herself; I mean different from the adult Robin. She would talk quietly with Lucy and cry on almost every visit. I had never before seen a new human mother, so had no frame of reference to determine whether this was normal or not. In contrast to Mira, who had stood up on her own promptly after exiting from Donkers's body, Jasmine was largely helpless and did require a significant amount of attention. That would surely be exhausting, so intense fatigue was potentially the reason for Robin's melancholy. Yet I sensed it was more complicated, that something else was going on.

At the next larger family gathering, Jasmine was placed on a blanket on the ground. I moved towards her and marveled at her crawling. She studied me and I her. I could see Robin, Wade, and

Nookomis in her face, especially in her dark eyes. I was looking forward to Jasmine growing from miniature to tiny so she could move around more on her own and we could undertake shared activities. I began to imagine our future together as I would show her the gardens, Takeo's pond, the mammals, the frogs, everything and everyone. I had witnessed girls becoming women. Now I was going to help a baby become a little girl.

"Can you move it away from Jasmine?" Easton called. He was standing nearby talking to a man I had seen at the wedding but not since.

"She's fine," Lucy said adamantly. *She* being me. *She* also being Jasmine.

Easton later regaled the crowd with stories from a recent boating experience. Jasmine began gurgling, then making soft and sporadic sounds, not words but the mighty seeds of words. Easton halted midsentence. "Can you just take her somewhere, babe. I'm trying to talk here."

Awkward air descended and filled the space immediately.

Wade stood up. "I can take her."

"No, no, you're gonna love this story," Easton said. Wade stayed standing and looked at Robin. But it was Easton who spoke to her. "Go for a walk or something."

Robin picked up the baby.

"I'll join you," Lucy said, and they walked off.

The awkward air swirled around and then moved on. The story about boating continued. I remember not a word of it, only how I felt.

Fifty suns later, or thereabouts, Aspen arrived poolside with Robin and Jasmine. Lucy and Wade came down from the residence, and they all gathered on the motion-picture-screening couches. Joan took Jasmine. "Come on, sweet baby girl. Let's enjoy some fresh air."

"It's nice to have some quiet," Robin said, then started to cry. "I'm sorry. I love Jasmine."

"Of course you do, sweetheart," Wade said. "No one would ever question that. There is nothing wrong with wanting a break from the exhaustion of a baby."

"I sound like a monster. I'm a bad mother."

"You are a great mother." Wade smiled. "Your patience reminds me of a particularly incredible mother, and grandmother. I see her in you all the time." Robin's face managed a small smile in return.

I had suspected and feared it to be true. I had not seen Nookomis in quite some time. I held her in my heart.

"I'm in awe of you," Aspen said. Her face was taut. "But I am worried about you."

"I appreciate that, but I'm okay. I can function without sleep."

"That's not what I mean."

"We're all worried about you," Lucy said.

Robin wiped tears off her cheeks more forcefully than expected. "What?"

There was silence. It was not exactly awkward. It was something else. Something hard to explain. Wade and Lucy looked at each other. I felt their anxiousness. It shot through me like a current. Lucy spoke first.

"Honey, we don't like how Easton speaks to you."

Robin's mouth opened in a silent gasp. "Excuse me?"

"You don't seem like yourself," Wade added.

Robin snorted. "I don't seem like myself? Maybe because I'm raising a friggin' baby here!"

"It's more than that. This isn't about you or anything you're doing," Lucy said, her calm tone a stark contrast to Robin's.

"What I am doing is working my ass off to be a good wife and mother."

"Absolutely you are. Does Easton appreciate it?"

"Of course he does. He has a ton of responsibility. You know exactly what that's like. How much a career can take over your mind and life."

"Does he say anything about how hard you work?" Wade asked.

"I'm just being a mother right now."

"A very difficult job, Robin, like you just explained," Aspen said.

"What, you want him to, like, say thank you to me or something?"

"Why not?" Wade said.

"Why not? Don't be ridiculous. This entire discussion is absurd and not what I thought was in store for me when you invited me over."

Lucy looked to be thinking, summoning something. "I just have to say this, Robin. I think Easton is crushing you."

Robin stared and then stood up sharply. "I can't believe you are all ganging up on me!"

She stormed towards Joan, who was near the mimosa trees with Jasmine. Robin took Jasmine and marched back to the residence. The anxiousness hung in place.

The sound of tires squealing.

Lucy, Wade, and Aspen sat in silence.

Robin and Jasmine did not return to this place for a significant amount of time. Their absence felt like a drought. Long ago I accepted that I would be confined to glimpses of human life, but during this period, I deeply wished I could reach indoors, and beyond these walls, to hear everything that was going on.

Then something changed out there. Robin changed something. She arrived with Jasmine and stayed. Easton was nowhere to be seen. Robin was calmer. So was I.

Jasmine had transformed from teeny-tiny bubbler to still-tiny-but-less-teeny human who could walk around on her own. She would wobble on occasion and lean on me to regain her balance. I was happy to be of assistance. She began to make music of a kind. She would sing to herself and sit among the flowers. I stayed with her, wrapping her in care and basking in her joy.

Robin's return was not the only major change that took place. Lucy resigned from the movie-making business. I say *resigned*, not *retired*, because although she was aging, she was hale. Fit and strong in body and mind. I knew she was not planning to spend the remainder of her life in a state of relaxation. Of course, I would have enjoyed such a turn of events for self-interested reasons, yet simultaneously, I knew Lucy's formidable mind and heart needed to be of service to the world beyond these walls.

She did spend nearly thirty suns here and she was really here; it was marvelous. She sat by the pool and listened to the birds, breathing deeply and rubbing my neck. She walked around the gardens with me like we were kids again. Although we were both more weathered, my love for Lucy was as pure as a spring redbud.

One golden hour we sat together in what had been the learning pod, and she studied me with more intensity than usual but did not say a word. I desperately wanted to know what she was thinking! It was even more annoying than listening to people on their portable telephones and only hearing one half of the conversation. All I could do was stare back at Lucy and lift each of my legs before letting them drop with more of a thud than usual. However, this only succeeded in making her laugh.

Robin and Jasmine often joined Lucy and me, and we would tour about, exploring and admiring trees and flowers. Even Wade, when he was not away fighting for the rivers, would come along. After everything that had happened, and everyone who had come and gone, it felt indescribably wonderful to be together, and to have a bouncy new member of the family I could help teach and nurture. I especially enjoyed Jasmine's songs and hearing her laugh, as well as seeing Robin return to a truer version of herself.

I cherished this time as I knew it would not last. Lucy was starting a business focused on finding as many ways as possible to make plants delicious (which seemed odd to me since plants are already delicious) and into protein. Robin was going to be leading a program focused on women in sports at a university in Los Angeles.

It became quiet again after they left. Lucy was as busy as she had been making movies. I spent a lot of time with the mammals. When mother and daughter came to visit, Jasmine would buzz around on her own with my dutiful supervision. She meandered among the flowers and plants, looking up at the trees, listening to the birds, trying to sing their songs herself and join the avian chorus. She even composed a song about me. It consisted primarily of her singing "Magic" repeatedly in different tones and at varied speeds, but it was splendid. Watching Jasmine grow was fascinating, and she was the very embodiment of possibility. Who would she become? What would she accomplish? She was already so caring and inquisitive. She was carrying the spirits of the many women in her life. This made me miss her even more when she was not here.

One golden hour, I spotted Lucy in the movie-screening area enjoying a rare moment of relaxation and set off in her direction. As I approached, I recognized one of the voices on the stereo. My twirling friend in a beautiful harmony. It made my heart sing. Lucy swayed gently with the music.

But a flash of movement caught her attention. It was Wade.

He was running towards us. Lucy sat right up straight, clearly confused. As he arrived, her body froze. Wade's shoulders were rising and falling with his breath, but he could not speak. His face, normally filled with levity, was gaunt.

Lucy stood up. "What's going on?" The panic was a tornado.

He shook his head and tried to speak but could only hide his eyes in his hand.

"What's happened?" Lucy was yelling. "What is going on, Wade?"

Wade shook his head no, but the answer was yes. Yes, there will be eternal devastation. Unfathomable consequences. Pain the severity of which you could never anticipate.

Wade spoke, but it was not his voice that emerged.

"No, no, no, no, no." Lucy started shaking. "No, no, this is not happening. This is not happening. This is not happening. No."

Easton had attacked Robin.

And Jasmine.

Jasmine was gone.

Chameleonic

IT WAS AS if an ocean of sadness crashed through the walls and submerged this place. There was a depth and heaviness to the sorrow that made it difficult to breathe. I knew Robin was here, but I did not see her for hundreds of suns. The girl who had spent endless days and evenings roaming, climbing, running, and swimming danced vibrantly in my mind as the woman stayed indoors. I remained around the residence, waiting in vain for a sign or symbol of Robin, or any word of what was going on. I heard vehicles come and go but I saw almost no people, save Leon, who moved quietly among the gardens.

Time both slowed down and sped up in this suspended state while my desolation remained consistent. I felt a fleeting moment of reprieve when a new dog arrived. He looked like Sunbeam but was darker, a mighty black-and-tan individual with pointy ears. He promptly registered my presence and walked over, sniffed my face and body, then returned to Wade. His name was Banjo and he had a strong, confident energy about him. Wade did not use a leash and Banjo never strayed farther than about twenty feet any which way.

Finally, one evening, Lucy, Aspen, and Wade sat behind the residence and Banjo lay nearby.

"I'm sorry you came all this way. I thought she'd be ready for a visitor," Lucy said. There was a chill in her voice that stood in such contrast to her usual warmth and animation.

"No, there's no need to apologize," Aspen said. "It's nice to see you two. Are you doing okay?"

Lucy shrugged. "*Okay* is a stretch, but we're trying. Let's talk about something else. How are you? You said you were going back to the archive?"

"Yeah, I did. There is a lot of material to sort through, so I don't have anything yet. I'd like to take Robin with me, when she's ready."

They sat in silence. Banjo suddenly stood up and trotted to the glass door. Lucy got up and opened it so he could enter the residence.

"He's really in tune with her. It's powerful to witness," Wade said, and his eyes filled with tears. Lucy wiped a tear off her own cheek and squeezed his arm as she sat back down.

"It comes in waves, you know," he said, his voice wavering. "I try to focus on work. It lets me put my mind in another space, almost like a separate room, and focus on the future. But then when things get quiet, I feel everything all over again. I relive each moment over and over again, not only in my mind, but the panic also surges through my body as if I'm just finding out. Then I feel guilty because it's not about me and—"

"Wade, you cannot think like that," Aspen said. "This is our tragedy."

"I feel it in my lungs most of all, a little or a lot, depending on the moment," Lucy said. "But the pain is never not there."

She wiped her face, but more tears fell.

Their agony was unbearable. Banjo reappeared at the window, peering outwards.

They say time heals. I am unsure. I have a unique relationship with time. I have considered this question from every angle. I remain uncertain.

Strange sounds woke me, and I promptly determined that their source was Poppy. Poof was lying on the ground in the shelter. Poof had died overnight. I hoped she had simply gone to sleep and felt no fear or pain. Leon buried her beside Zedonk. He placed stones to mark both of their final resting places. I lay nearby. Poof had been with me since the latter days of Ralph's life. I still remembered our initial encounter vividly, Poof's pronounced teeth and glamorous hairdo. Most importantly, I remembered her immediately positive outlook and care for Eeyore. Mira, Donkers, and Eeyore spent the next suns and moons right up close to Poppy. I hoped I, too, was providing some comfort, that my presence offered reassurance and love, despite our vast physical differences.

Undoubtedly, I looked stoic to anyone observing, but the truth is I was overwhelmed with sadness. There was altogether too much death. It felt like an unrelenting onslaught of tragedies. When there is life, there is inevitably death. But an intellectual acknowledgment of this fact, a rational awareness of its certainty, offers no actual comfort.

When the days started to get cooler, I realized something significant. I had maintained a very compact range between the mammals' quadrant and the back of the residence, venturing no farther in any direction. The entire summer had passed. I had not laid any eggs. I had felt no need. My body had produced no eggs.

During this extended period, I often considered what I would do when Robin finally emerged, and wondered how badly she was injured. I thought she might sit on the patio or even simply look through the glass doors before crossing the threshold back into the outdoor world, that there might be steps or stages she would follow to slowly reintroduce herself to the space that had nurtured her and Jasmine.

Yet without warning, Robin appeared outside one afternoon with Banjo right at her side. She walked with a cane and descended the steps behind the residence, then proceeded towards the fountain. She passed it and continued onwards. She was about to step onto the grassy area that led to the small house, what had been the Yamadas' home. It was empty, and I do not believe she had visited it since Lily and her family had moved away. At that point, Robin became unable to proceed, to cross into the open space behind and beyond the residence. Her eyes filled with tears. She retraced her steps, all the way back into the residence, and disappeared from view once again.

Two suns later, she and Banjo attempted to follow the same route. This time, Robin did not make it past the fountain. I felt certain the difficulty was not related to pain of the physical variety. I have taken many a lengthy journey wherein the primary challenge was emotional, not a matter of distance or literal terrain.

I had felt utterly useless during this entire period, unable to offer even any semblance of support to Robin. That could now change. I positioned myself at the very back of the residence's domain, two legs on the stones and two on the soil that led to the small house. I remained there for five suns and was prepared for longer, when Robin reinitiated her journey, her eyes focused entirely on me. As she got closer, I swung myself around and set off towards the small house. She walked beside me and Banjo beside her. I surged ahead and did not hesitate. We marched together in lockstep.

She walked right up and opened the door, then stepped inside. When Robin reemerged, she smiled.

"Thank you, Daisuke Magic."

Robin proceeded to walk around daily, periodically returning to the small house, but also venturing all around this place and making notes. I went along and felt her gaining strength, in all senses of the word. Banjo would always join us. Banjo seemed strong, but I wondered how he felt, helping people who had experienced such profound grief, whether his work weighed him down at times. Banjo was very dedicated, that was clear, and I am certain he took pride in his place at Robin's side. I wished I could communicate significant feelings as he did, and as Sunbeam had, to express the love I felt unequivocally every day. Robin was still faster than me but would adjust her pace so that I could keep up. Here I was working to assist her, and she was thinking of me.

As some social activity recommenced, I was able to ascertain crucial information about what was being planned. The little house was to become Robin and Banjo's home. Robin was going to be overseeing a new venture: People were going to come here for healing.

Initially, I did not fully understand what this would entail, but I knew I would help as much as tortoisely possible.

Robin's initiative was called Harmony Ridge, a worthy name that would have made Melvin smile. A new shelter was erected at the base of the pool. Assorted smaller structures were scattered around the place, but I was pleased that they caused minimal disturbance to the flora and fauna. They seemed integrated, not imposed. What had been the cage area was demolished completely and then refashioned into a multilevel garden complete with a water feature and surrounded by rosebuds. The end of the cages felt truly monumental, and I watched their removal firsthand as many emotions and memories hurtled through me.

I was particularly delighted because the sides of this cage-replacing garden structure sloped, and I was able to enter and drink. I tried it out immediately and then remained within it, enjoying the not-quite-bird's-eye view but still elevated vantage point it offered. Banjo even climbed up with me, and Robin took photos. I am certain we looked enchanting together.

The first few hundred suns revealed what became, more or less, the norm. Smaller groups of mostly but not exclusively women would come and engage in different activities often led by Robin or her new collaborator, Summer, a lovely person befitting of her name who moved and spoke as though wrapped in a relaxing breeze. There was art, which would have warmed Lily's spirit. There were deliberate walks in specific areas, and peaceful moments within gardens. They would eat plants, never animals. Sometimes the guests would groom the donkeys, and Poppy would stand there surveying the entire situation, overseeing everyone. She was slowing down. So was Donkers. Eeyore was really slowing down. They still gave generously of their time and patience to help these people, though. Leon proudly wore a smart turquoise shirt that said "Harmony Ridge" across his heart.

For the one-year anniversary of Harmony Ridge, a garden was planted in memory and honor of Jasmine. It included a delicate blanket of white jasmine flowers and others that were the favorites of the pollinators, the butterflies and bees who had so delighted little Jasmine. Robin would often enter the garden and sit on the ground as profound emotions emanated from within her. I would stand at her side, trying to wrap her in unity and quiet comfort.

The first years of Harmony Ridge primarily involved adults, but one day a group of children arrived. These children did not speak with spoken words; they spoke with their hands. While many of the guests of Harmony Ridge were in pain and came here to try to heal and find joy once again, this group did not seem to be damaged at all. These children were here to explore and experience.

Robin and Summer spoke aloud with the accompanying adults, who served as translators for some of the activities. At other times, the children moved around on their own, in the sort of vivacious and exuberant manner that only children embody. They had vigorous discussions about flowers, trees, and me. They studied a lone bee who delicately traveled among the flowers of the Jasmine memorial garden. Some of the children rubbed my neck and back, tentatively at first and then with more enthusiasm. One boy was startled when he first saw me, while another seemed hostile. But other children spoke with these two and changed their perspectives. In one way, I have no idea what specifically was discussed. Yet another part of me knew exactly what they were saying.

"The children want to know more about the . . . turtle?" the interpreter said.

Robin smiled. "The tortoise, absolutely. Her name is Magic."

The interpreter told the children, whose eyes became larger. They smiled and nodded, then asked another question.

"They are wondering where she is from."

"Well, we are working on figuring that out, actually," Robin replied. "I was at the archives with my cousin last week."

The children nodded.

"They think that's a good idea. And that she is beautiful."

One girl put both of her hands forward in loose fists, made small circles, then opened her palms to the earth. All the children did the same. The interpreter smiled.

"What is that sign?" Robin asked.

"Magic."

I watched as Robin practiced the sign, and my heart shimmered. After they were gone, I climbed up into the new elevated garden and surveyed this place. I saw new angles, shades, and textures I had never before noticed. I remained there for many suns and moons, reflecting. I also noted that Robin had mentioned archives. Aspen had spoken of them too, but I had not understood what that meant.

When I eventually descended, Summer and Robin were near the pool, preparing for the next group. There was some tension in the air, and Robin especially seemed to be engaged in her own existential period of reflection.

"I just don't know if we're doing enough," she said.

"We can't do everything."

"No, and we always knew that, but I feel like we're too limited."

"Do you want to do more for kids?"

"I've been thinking about who can afford to come here."

Summer nodded. "Ah. Yeah. I hear you."

"I can't ask Lucy for any more money."

"We could develop a plan to identify specific donors who could cover the costs for people who wouldn't normally be able to afford something like this."

"Maybe. But then who gets to decide which people are worthy of that charity? Can we even reach those who are really struggling, who would need this opportunity the most?"

"It's a tough situation, Robin. Let's think more about it, okay?"

The depth of Robin's heart reminded me so much of Lucy, who, unfortunately, I rarely saw. Until she appeared with a truly extraordinary human being, proving, once again, that Lucy kept holding me in her heart, and kept her word, wherever she was.

She Shells Sanctuary

I WAS NAPPING in the elevated garden when a woman marched right up to me with Lucy and Robin and began pointing things out about my body. She referred to my back as like a saddle that allowed me to reach higher plants (I certainly enjoy vegetation of all sizes). She stated that I am female (obviously) and specifically "large for a female," a splendid compliment indeed. She noted that my sturdiness would minimize the risk of toppling over if on highly uneven terrain (a frightful thought). She held my face in her hands, which was somewhat disagreeable, but I tolerated it. She scraped skin off my leg and placed the contents into a small container. Then she caused a sharp prick on the side of my neck, which I certainly did not enjoy, but it ended quickly.

With that poke, clarity and certainty arrived. This was a tortoise doctor. I had a doctor! What a momentous occasion!

"A real beauty," the doctor—my doctor—said, rubbing my neck.

Not only had Lucy brought me a doctor, but she also had mango, and they both offered me slices.

"I'll be back in touch when I know more," my doctor said. "This is a top priority, but the process still takes time."

A good number of suns, fifty or more, passed as I waited anxiously to see what my doctor had discovered, to no avail. I decided to keep busy in order to manage my impatience. I found Leon, Lucy, and a woman I did not recognize near the mammals and immediately saw why. It was Eeyore. It was as though his body was shutting down. The woman helped Eeyore into the shelter and examined his body. She allowed Donkers, Mira, and Poppy to approach and nuzzle him, then they were placed in the adjacent field.

We watched Eeyore take his last breaths, and his body fall still. Poppy died a few suns later; perhaps her heart had cracked once again to the point that it broke. Leon buried them both alongside Zedonk and Poof. There was so much history under that soil, at the base of those trees, the physical reminders of lives, of residents, of the thoughtful beings with whom I had moved through life.

What happened next, I could never have anticipated. Two new birds were brought here. They were unlike any birds I had ever seen before. They were not placed in cages. They were free birds, but also different from those whose songs and colors adorned the branches and canopies. These birds pecked the ground and used their delicate legs to dig gently in the grass and soil. But most of their feathers had been rubbed off.

"I admit that I haven't seen many chickens who are alive, but I didn't expect bald patches like that," Max said when he first saw them. He was a new man in Robin's life. I had a good initial impression of him based on observation of his comportment on a few prior occasions.

"That's from the cages."

He nodded. "I'm glad you could help them." He put his arm around Robin and pointed to the donkeys. "What are their names?"

"Donkers and Mira. Mother and daughter. They've been here basically as long as we have."

"Wow. Speaking of, have you heard anything more from the scientist—" Max tilted his head towards me.

"The herpetologist."

"You really need to be careful with that word. Don't want anyone getting the wrong impression."

Robin laughed. "Nothing yet."

Herpetologist. What a magnificent word. *Her-pe-tol-o-gist.* My doctor was a herpetologist.

"Peace and Freedom," Robin said, looking back to the chickens. "That's what I'd like to name the hens. Peace and Freedom."

"Sounds perfect."

I was absolutely mesmerized by the hens and stayed near them as they began to explore, although they never ventured too far. Admittedly, their arrival distracted me somewhat from the still very raw pain of losing Eeyore and Poppy. These birds were survivors; of what I was not entirely sure. They stuck close together, but one was more boisterous, while the other had a stronger sense of stillness in her demeanor. I felt she was Peace, and the former Freedom.

They made the most incredible sound as they foraged, this gentle purr. At times, they would sing me into midday slumber, like a lullaby. One afternoon, Freedom found a dime. (Although I am no businesstortoise, as previously established, and rarely see the mechanics of money exchanging hands, I am aware of what a dime looks like.) It caused quite a frenzy. They both pecked and pecked at it, with Peace doing a little hop, seemingly enamored with the dime's sheen. Freedom even picked it up and carried it around. I feared she might mistake it for food, but she saw it as a shiny treasure.

Slowly, some of their feathers returned, first as little fuzzy nubs. I wondered what Preciosa would make of them, and vice versa, if they had the opportunity to meet. I felt certain Prince would have sought to show off his plumage and impress them, not intending to mock the absence of theirs, but rather to find affinity. I thought of all the different birds who had been brought to this place, in their diversity and unity.

The hens slept in the shelter every night. During the golden hour, they would make their way to the shelter and use their feet to dig a little hole in the straw, and then tuck in together. They went to bed early. I started doing the same so that I could rise with them. I wondered whether they had nightmares about their former life, which had taken their feathers, or happy dreams about the bugs and seeds they had eaten that day and the dime. I was curious about whether they would move out into the trees as they gained confidence. I thought they would look magnificent and regal resting on a branch.

One morning, there was a soft rain, and they remained in the shelter for longer, pecking around in the straw. As the rain dried up, everyone emerged, and the hens began their daily ritual. Out of nowhere, a massive bird flew down from the sky, picked up Peace, and flew away with her. The violence of it sucked all the air from my lungs. Freedom wailed with fear and ran towards the shelter at top speed. I stood helplessly, wondering whether Peace had been killed instantly in the aerial assault or was feeling terror soaring through the sky in the grip of another.

That evening, Robin came down and noticed the absence. She walked around, frantically looking for Peace, then sat and cried.

Lucy returned with Robin two suns later, and they leaned against the fence. "It would be so sad," Robin said.

"In some ways, yes. But you can visit them. It's supposed to be an incredible place. The staff are experts."

"And there are other donkeys? Because when Donkers dies, Mira is going to be devastated."

"The woman said there are six donkeys. Plus other rescued chickens, sheep, cows. Mira will probably make new friends right away. They both will."

"But what if the move really stresses them out?" Robin wiped away a tear. "This has been their home for so long."

"Honey, the woman I spoke with was confident it would be the best choice for all three of them. This place is fine, but they deserve more. You know, when I was a little girl, there was a monkey here who was alone and so sad. Someone very special to me helped find a new home for her with other monkeys and trees, and room to move. I like to think it was a kind of sanctuary. A protosanctuary maybe. These animals can be in a real safe haven too."

I had seen how large the fields some animals called home were in motion pictures. I could imagine them. Vast stretches of land with grasses and gently rolling hills where animals who happen to like to run can gallivant around to their hearts' content. If Mira had the opportunity to be in such a place, she should be. If Donkers could spend her final suns and moons in wide-open spaces, she should. And Freedom unequivocally needed better. She had been through far, far too much already in her short lifetime. She needed a community of other chickens.

Robin took a deep breath, then spoke. "You're right. They are owed the best we can provide."

People came to take Freedom, Mira, and Donkers to their new home. I was happy for my friends, I truly was. Their departure was still painful. I had conveyed my love and good wishes earlier that day and preferred to observe at a bit of distance.

The people were kind. They were careful with the donkeys and especially with Freedom.

"Her name is perfect," the woman said. "We will honor it every day."

Unbirthdays

I ENTERED AND then remained in a period of prolonged reflection after their departure. Had I considered this place a sanctuary? No, its identity was more complicated. How this place was understood and experienced varied depending on who was doing the understanding and experiencing. And when.

I believe the donkeys were happy here, the alpacas too. Admittedly, they were quite stoic, the donkeys in particular. I could not help but wonder if they secretly longed for more space and stimulation, which would not have been unreasonable in the least. Maybe they were content rather than happy.

I thought often of Peace, a life cut short, after she had only but tasted liberty. I wished I had been able to learn more about her and stand at her side in solidarity as she finally experienced a real opportunity to control her own body and movement. I pictured Freedom among other hens, and hoped they were welcoming her with judiciousness and care, and that occasionally she might stumble across a shiny object that would bring her delight. I hoped she, Donkers, and Mira would spend their remaining days in the full rainbows of vibrancy and love.

I listened to the songs of the free birds, watched rabbits forage, and reminded myself that I was part of this community. The free animals and me, our peaceful accord was well established, as was our willingness, nay, enthusiasm for coexistence, despite our great diversity.

However, I could not help but wonder: Was this the right place for me? Lucy felt other animals, even those who had not been taken from their homelands, deserved better homes. Yet I was still here, the only tortoise in this place.

Every other animal brought here was gone, other than Banjo. The gray that had spread across his muzzle and eyebrows was handsome and distinguished, although I knew what it represented. As a dog he had a special status and lifestyle, and seemed to relish being almost entirely with people, but I wondered if he quietly wished for canine companionship too.

It was Banjo's voice that summoned me from the forest and my mental labyrinth. He was barking with a hearty timbre at quite a volume. I spotted him, Robin, and a group of guests who had been sitting in a circle but were now standing in a huddle. The reason for Banjo's ferocity was in plain sight. There was a man standing near a smaller cluster of trees, staring at them. I did not recognize this man, and I most certainly did not care for his lewd behavior. Robin swiftly guided the guests towards the residence. Banjo followed her but kept turning around to bark at the strange man, who remained unmoved. As they retreated, Leon arrived with police! The man tried to flee, but they tackled him to the ground and then walked him away.

It was disturbing. This place is most secure, the walls substantial obstacles for anyone who wishes to enter through a means other than the requisite front gate. The smaller gate that Takeo had used was similarly secure. I remained uncertain about how this man had gotten in and what he wanted, but knew it was not welcome.

I was not the only one troubled by this turn of events. By the time I reached the pool, intense dialogue was taking place. Robin, Summer, Leon, and Wade had all gathered and were discussing what would happen next.

"The ceremony is in two days, and this asshole has to ruin everything," Robin said through tears.

"We can postpone," Summer said.

"I don't know. I don't think so. It's not like it's easy to book the governor and everyone else."

"You could change the nature of the event," Wade suggested. "Do something different?"

Robin shook her head. "I appreciate that. I appreciate you. I appreciate all of you. But it's fine. I'm fine."

I knew she was not fine. It was written all over her face and permeated the sound of her voice, despite her best attempts. I do not believe anyone thought she was truly fine.

I was unsure where to go. It is not that I did not know my options, of course. The issue was that I did not know where I wanted to go. I had always moved in pursuit of my preferred food options or to seek coolness, but most of all, to be with others. To provide support as best as I could, to listen, watch, and learn. Now there were so few others. I considered turning around and going right back to the forest sanctuary. But it was hot. And I can admit I was a bit spooked by the strange man too.

I opted to move towards the mimosa trees. Their beauty did not disappoint. There I remained, and being among the bright pinks and greens brought thoughts of Lily. What had Lily done after she left this place? What had she accomplished? How were Ayame and Michio? How was Melvin? How was Eliana? Even Emmet. I began thinking about everyone who had left. Everyone who was gone.

I imagined a whole host of possible lives for Lily and was picturing her in an art gallery when Leon and Max arrived with a wheelbarrow. "One, two, three" and they tried to lift. Me. They tried to lift me. The mere prospect is uproarious!

Needless to say, they did not succeed. They returned with Summer and Wade, who was still mighty, despite his advancing age. "One, two, three . . . good god" and I was airborne, then placed into the wheelbarrow. We were all fortunate that my impressive corpus was able to be contained within it, although my front legs were maneuvered so that they emerged out the front. I was propped right up and expect I looked striking.

"Precious cargo," Wade said.

"I will be very careful," Leon replied.

With a good amount of effort, he was able to lift the handle portions of the wheelbarrow and then begin moving it slowly and me along with it. It had been a long time since I had been shuttled around in a chariot of this sort. I remembered my initial ride vividly and how Takeo had driven me with immense care to the learning pod, where I was able to launch into the universe of the mind.

"You all right in there?" Leon asked.

I certainly was. Despite my expanded girth, I felt quite comfortable and most enjoyed the view of this place as we smoothly moved across it. Beyond the pool, there was a new post or tree of some sort covered in a dark green cloth in the adjacent garden, and that was our destination. He parked the wheelbarrow nearby—remarkably, almost exactly where I had been standing when I had been placed in the wheelbarrow the first time, when I was much younger and smaller, and lifting me required the strength of only two people.

"One, two, three, Christ, this is harder" had me soaring again. I was placed on the ground with a little more thud than I believe was planned but was physically unscathed. I contemplated the rationale for my relocation. A ceremony. Yes, there had been the discussion of a ceremony. It seemed perfectly reasonable that the pleasure of my company would be sought for this pending special social occasion.

What could the ceremony be for? An anniversary? A major achievement?

I continued to consider possibilities as the pink-gray light of dusk set in and I drifted into slumber.

The following day I was awakened by a flurry of footsteps. *Flurry* makes it sound like these were rabbits or squirrels, though, and these were most certainly not small and spritely mammals. It was stomping that woke me; that is a more apt description. Largely indistinguishable mammals—men in dark suits and sunglasses—were again on the premises, moving here and there, to and fro. Leon rolled through and primped and primed some of the closest flowers, then departed.

Robin. Summer. Max. Wade. Aspen. People I did not know. They were all milling about. Then two women and a man in a wheelchair parked near the edge. A man who was very thin. It was Michio. Michio, Lily, and Ayame! I was overjoyed to see the Yamadas again but filled with worry. Lily came right over, wheeling her dad.

"Hello, my beautiful friend," she said, kneeling down in front of me.

I reached my nose forward, and she gently touched me. Michio smiled, his face so different, but his warmth the same.

A man in a suit who seemed strangely familiar arrived. Lily wheeled Michio back towards Ayame. I desperately wanted them to stay with me, but the man in the suit was commanding everyone's attention. I could not place where I knew him from. Of course, the answer is I knew him from here, but what I mean is that I did not know when I had seen him, why he had been here, or who he was. A small crowd formed, including people carrying large cameras. Leon and all the women from the house stood at the back. Then Lucy appeared, and she was with my doctor! I was feeling so many conflicting emotions.

The familiar yet unnamed man stood facing the crowd, as did my doctor, Lucy, and Robin, who stepped in front of the microphone.

"Ladies and gentlemen, distinguished guests, Governor."

The man nodded, and I realized who he was. I had not met this man in person—I had seen him in motion pictures.

"My name is Robin Reed, and I am pleased to welcome you to Harmony Ridge for this truly historic day. It's a story that may seem right out of a Hollywood film"—the crowd chuckled—"yet I assure you, this tale is entirely real. I'd like to invite the incredible Lucy Harrington to tell you more about it."

Lucy squeezed Robin's hand.

"Good morning, everyone, and thank you for coming. This beautiful property, now home to the inspiring work of Harmony Ridge, has also been my family's residence for more than a few decades. When my late uncle, Ralph Chilton, purchased it in 1946, he inherited all who were already within these walls, but let's just say he did not know much about them, never mind the details of their stories.

"When I came here as a little girl, I instantly became friends with one of the most extraordinary residents. Well, flash forward to today—please pardon the pun—and that resident is still here, this tortoise who you see right here." She gestured towards me. "It has taken a long time to uncover the truth about her, far longer than it should have. There were phone calls made to zoos, museums, and universities. My wonderful niece, Aspen"—Lucy pointed at Aspen, who waved—"spent hours in the archives digging through dusty boxes and files, trying to fill in the blanks."

"Robin helped," Aspen called.

Lucy nodded. "Absolutely. It took a lot of brain power, co-operation, and persistence. Thanks to a series of suggestions, we eventually met Dr. Lorna Lambeau of Marshall University and now can benefit from her scientific expertise, which, and I think this is crucial, she combines with a deep sense of care and a strong moral compass. She has extraordinary information to share."

My doctor nodded emphatically and moved to the microphone. "It's an absolute pleasure," she said. "Thank you."

My heart was racing.

"Ladies and gentleman, this magnificent creature here, she is the oldest tortoise in North America. This tortoise is one hundred and ten years old, give or take a year."

The entire crowd gasped and stared at me. They applauded, and for good reason. I was 110 years old!

"By combining DNA testing with the archival records, we have determined with near certainty that she was brought to California as a youngster in 1901 after being originally intended for Lord Walter Rothschild's private collection in Cambridge, England. Unfortunately, it included animals like emus, kangaroos, zebras who were trained to pull a carriage, and more than one hundred and forty giant tortoises. He was known to ride around on top of them."

"How did the tortoise end up here?" someone from the crowd asked.

Lucy stepped back in front of the microphone. "How she ended up within these walls is the only piece of the mystery we cannot solve. Someone brought her here instead of shipping her to England. We can speculate about who that was and their reasons, but do not know who or why for certain."

Lucy took a deep breath. "There is even more to her story. This individual is a Galápagos giant tortoise, but she is not simply any Galápagos tortoise. Dr. Lambeau has established that this is a Fernandina tortoise, a species long thought extinct." Lucy looked right at me. "But here she is, the last remaining Fernandina tortoise on the planet."

Everything was a blur. I heard more gasps. Loud ones.

Then Lucy: "This tortoise has had many names, but we want to give her one more, one that honors her homeland. Today, we adorn her"—Lucy looked at me—"you, with the name Fernandita as a tribute to Fernandina Island, where you were meant to be."

I thought I was going to pass out right then and there.

The man took to the microphone. "It is my pleasure as governor to recognize this incredible story and afford this tortoise the official protection of the State of California as a living monument to history, a history that has not always recognized or respected animals."

The governor pulled the cloth off the post and revealed a plaque with writing and a lovely etching of a tortoise. Everyone applauded. He reached down and handed me a slice of mango, which, of course, I still managed to devour, despite the state of shock I was in.

A woman from the crowd spoke. "A lovely gesture, Governor, but why not send the tortoise back to the Galápagos Islands now, given all the advances in conservation? I'm thinking of Lonesome George."

The governor looked to Dr. Lambeau and Lucy. Dr. Lambeau stepped to the microphone.

"For those who don't know, Lonesome George is the last remaining Pinta tortoise who currently still lives in the Galápagos.

We certainly did consider whether Fernandita could be returned. I consulted extensively with colleagues, especially those in Ecuador who are on the front lines of tortoise conservation, and we ultimately decided it was not wise. The travel and seismic change would be risky for Fern herself, and given that she has been away from the region for more than a century, there were concerns about what the impacts of the reintroduction would be on tortoises there, particularly the potential exposure to foreign pathogens. So, we decided that all things and beings considered, at this point in history, this is the best place for her, the safest for everyone."

The governor returned to the microphone.

"Fernandita joins a special group of tortoises, among them Jonathan, who lives on the grounds of the governor on the island of Saint Helena and is believed to be the oldest land animal on Earth at around one hundred eighty years young!" The audience gasped once again. "As for Fern here, this next chapter took some interesting negotiations, which I was pleased to support directly, including discussions with the governor of Tennessee, and the results are really something. For more than a century, this tortoise has been alone." He was technically incorrect, but I was intellectually functional enough despite the explosion of emotions erupting within me to know what he meant. "Well, that ends today."

A group of people in khaki uniforms appeared wheeling a large box. They pushed and pulled it until it was near me, opened its front, and stepped back. Nothing happened. Everyone sat in silence, watching and waiting, with bated breath.

From within the box, a beautiful face peered out. Then a strong leg stepped forward, followed by another.

A tortoise!

"Ladies and gentlemen—and Fernandita, of course—may I present the newest resident of Harmony Ridge, an Aldabra giant tortoise named Vida."

People cheered. The noise did not startle Vida, and she continued to extract her gorgeous self from within the box, walking directly towards me. I moved towards her, and we touched noses. It felt like she was hugging my heart. The governor handed us each a slice of mango. I watched her devour the treat in a most enthusiastic manner. It was delightful. No wonder people enjoy watching me eat.

I know little of what else happened. Things were said in my—in *our*—vicinity that entered my ears but not my brain, or my conscious brain anyway. All I know is that Vida and I stared at each other. Then Vida started to eat a nearby plant, and I continued to stare at her. She (rightly) seemed impressed with me but as though she had seen other tortoises before. Who were they? Where had she been?

Clara danced into my mind, her voice a clarion call.

"Dos gardenias para ti. Con ellas quiero decir te quiero, te adoro, mi vida."

Two gardenias for you. With them I wish to say I love you, I adore you, my life.

My Vida.

In one of Lucy's motion pictures, this is where the tale would end. There would be a triumphant musical crescendo or, at minimum, a catchy closing-credit earworm. But my story, which is our story, does not end here.

Mi Vida

THE SUBSEQUENT SUNS were a new level of vibrancy as Vida and I moved around together. We began an extensive period of exploration and traversed every inch of this place so she could become acquainted with all the intricate details and sample the many culinary offerings.

When she first tasted the exquisiteness of the prickly pear cactus flower, Vida was so thrilled she spoke. It was unlike anything I had ever heard and yet I immediately understood and responded in kind. It was extraordinary. We were able to convey our moods and interests, and I relished being able to both feel and hear her. What I could not glean, however, were additional details about her past. I could only understand her present and share her future, but I was overwhelmingly grateful for both.

Through Vida, it was almost as though I was seeing this place anew, the brilliance of its green lyricism and floral punctuation marks. Delight radiated from deep within her. I listened to the free birds' songs with a renewed sense of purpose and bliss through her ears and my own.

Yet there were fewer of them. That was undeniable. Some songs I had heard in the past were no longer part of the music of this landscape. Other choruses endured but were smaller, quieter. The frogs, too, they and their songs were almost completely gone.

It was hot and dry, and we moved around carefully and deliberately. There was smoke in the air. I have seen many a fire, either in a pit in the ground or, later on, literally in a table (and I do mean literally). I never got too close, or even really anywhere near their intense heat, but their fragrance wafted through my nostrils. Robin had hosted more than a few round-the-fire sing-alongs, the repertoire ranging from the timeless (and thus tortoise-like?) Dolly Parton to the regal Beyoncé. One night, Robin's guests had even created a delightful a cappella version of "Single Ladies" and then played the real song since one of them was adamant that she knew the entire choreography (I cannot confirm whether she did or not, but I found her dancing most impressive).

No, this smoke was different. It came from well beyond these walls. It hung heavily in the air and blocked the sun for many, well, suns. But Vida wanted to keep moving and relished having the opportunity to stretch out and move at a pace of our own choosing.

Vida was even taller than me, though she was younger. We were quite a pair of giants! I knew the latter fact because Dr. Lambeau recognized me as the oldest tortoise in America. I was more than a century old. I had been alive for the entirety of the twentieth century and now a decade into the twenty-first century.

The other news Lucy had shared was not joyful in the least, and I deliberately postponed considering it and instead focused on Vida. Guests of Harmony Ridge would invariably find us and marvel at our very existence but did not linger long. This was tortoise time in all senses of the word *time*.

The person who found us most often was Lucy, and I thought of her as an honorary tortoise anyway. She would walk around the gardens and sit quietly with us. Vida felt the power of my love for Lucy and understood that our union was possible because of her. Vida loved Lucy too. We would rest on either side of her in the shade, a living harmony.

Like me, Vida enjoyed the elevated garden, and after many hundreds of suns of exploration and enjoyment, we climbed up there and surveyed the beauty of this place together. It was only then that I began to think carefully about the full implications of what Lucy had shared at the ceremony about me. Fernandina tortoise. Believed to be extinct. Other than me.

It was a tragedy the likes of which are hard to accurately ~~capture~~ describe and explain. I had a homeland, an island named Fernandina. Tortoises had lived there. Giant, hearty, and hardy tortoises like me. My parents. My siblings, nieces, nephews, who, if science is correct (which it is whether you believe it to be or not), could have still been alive, too, had people behaved differently. Potential Fernandina tortoise friends and chosen family members would have been on this earth.

But now there were no Fernandina tortoises there. There were none of us anywhere, except me, here. One surviving member of an entire kind of being, far away from our ancestral lands. Vida shared her calmest energy to help me while I processed this information and its implications.

It took many suns for me to properly wrap my mind around it all. I could not reproduce. The days of my egg laying were gone and could not be summoned. Moreover, Vida was, of course, not capable of creating baby tortoises with me. Something that had been said in a side conversation on that most extraordinary day wiggled to the surface of my mind: "The zoo wanted to send a male, but we were worried he would mount Fern and hurt her."

First, what a randy bunch, we tortoises are!

But since this unknown male was not a Fernandina tortoise,

I do not know if he would have been able to help create any Fernandina tortoises. There were other giant tortoises thriving in our homeland, or at least near it. There had been talk of *islands*, plural. Those tortoises were being protected there, where they belong. Where we belong. That was significant news. I tried to focus on that and on the idea of them. The reality of them.

But the question of motherhood kept resurfacing in my mind. I was not physically able to help create a Fernandina tortoise. My egg-laying days had disappeared with the twentieth century, the same year Jasmine was stolen. Since Vida and I had been roaming, I had not seen a lot of Robin up close, and my mind dwelled on her well-being. I hoped she had been pleased with how the ceremony had gone, and that she was feeling hopeful.

As for me, I had never wanted to be a mother. But if I had known there was no one else like me left on this entire planet, I might have changed my mind. I could have weighed the options carefully, the pros and cons, the possibilities and limitations of what I could offer, and where I was, and what could happen here, and what it would mean for the possible new tortoise life. I could have decided.

But I did not get to choose. Some men whose faces I did not see and whose names I do not know got to make that decision about my body and my life. The impact of their choices have affected an entire group and our very trajectory on this earth.

Dr. Lambeau came to check on Vida and me every three hundred suns or so. We were well and Lucy made sure of that. We roamed and napped, and the work of Harmony Ridge continued with our support. Aspen became more involved. Her writing groups would often sit near us and work on their word and imagination exercises. Vida loved to help, and I enjoyed being a muse once again.

"The biography of a tortoise," someone announced during one such session.

"The autobiography!" offered another.

"I don't know if the publishing industry is quite ready for that," a third person said.

"Maybe a thriller about a surly detective who discovers a drug cartel is smuggling cocaine through tortoise shells?"

If you watched closely with an incisive eye, as I did, it was clear that Robin had never quite been the same after that man broke in. His violation of this sanctified space affected how she understood and moved through it. She kept working but seemed unsettled. Banjo slowed down, and then we all had to say goodbye. He had served Robin heroically during her most difficult and painful time and was buried beside Sunbeam. Two more remarkable beings who had been part of this place, this family and chosen family.

It took time, but Robin chose a different path and home. She decided to run to become part of the government. She said she wanted to help in a different way, especially people who could not afford to live near places like this or pay for the help they provided.

Summer and Aspen focused on Harmony Ridge, while Robin worked outside these walls. Then party-planning people started to come by. They set up tables for guests and a stage. The men in suits and sunglasses were back, surveying every inch of this place, and there was even a woman among them. As the sun descended, musicians appeared with instruments! Vida would experience her first traveling symphony!

When guests began arriving, I could not believe my ears. I would know that laugh anywhere. It was the epitome of song, like the man himself. He was older and somehow even more stylish. He and Lucy shook hands but then hugged. He laughed with his whole body when he saw me. When he was introduced to Vida, he became quiet. He looked right at me and smiled, nodding.

Vida and I parked ourselves directly in front of the stage, and this time, I knew we would not be asked to move to the side. We had front-row seats to witness all the incredible women who spoke with such eloquence about the future. I was deeply moved by Robin. I had never seen her so formidable. The power of her voice and conviction and fortitude would have soared even without a microphone.

Then, the stage went dark. A spotlight lit up the piano. Melvin sat down. The instant he touched the keys, I knew. He had played this song many, many nights, when it was just him and me. When he was sad, and when he was hopeful. Change was coming.

The light expanded, and there they were. The strings. The horns. The sound wrapped around us and held us together.

As the days got cooler and shorter, Vida and I stayed right in the hearth, needing to learn as much as possible about what was going on outside these walls. The energy was unlike anything I had ever felt before. It was excitement, but also tension, and they were inextricably linked. They could not be unwoven or even pried apart.

"Whatever happens tomorrow, I need you to understand how deeply grateful I am for you. Not just your unwavering support, but you as human beings, the most admirable of people," Robin said. "Everyone, please raise a glass to my father, imbaabaa, and my chosen mother."

Lucy's eyes glistened as the small group toasted, and Wade squeezed her hand.

"Even after everything I've witnessed, the losses and the progress alike, I can't believe we have reached this moment of possibility," Lucy said.

"To the power of women, and a more just future," Wade said, raising his glass. "May tomorrow make herstory right to the Oval Office."

After the guests were gone, Lucy and Wade hugged Robin, who then left. Wade and Lucy sat together on the couch quietly. Lucy smiled, stood up, and moved to the records. She selected one from long ago, then reached her hands out towards Wade.

They danced in the moonlight. The song took my breath away. "Sara."

They did not know.

They did not know that like so much that is truly beautiful, this song was nurtured here.

When it was over, Lucy wanted to stay out a little longer. Wade kissed her and walked towards their home.

Lucy chose a lounger near the learning pod. Vida and I moved too, placing ourselves on either side of her. Her arm reached out and stroked my neck. She stared up at the stars and breathed deeply. It was the epitome of peacefulness.

Then her head dropped. Her arm jerked away. She twitched sharply. I reached towards her with my nose, but her body was shaking.

Her life flashed before my eyes.

The little girl on the swing and hiding around the corner, listening to lessons intended for her brother.

The soaked young woman pulling me from the pool.

Her tearful smile when she sat with me on the ground, in what had finally become her home.

The triumph in her voice as she shared my story with the whole world.

Her dancing in the moonlight with Wade, the love of her life.

The other love of her life.

Lucy! Lucy! Lucy! Lucy . . .

She became still and looked right into my eyes. She smiled.

Then she was gone.

Flipped

I COULD LEARN every language on Earth and would still lack the words needed to explain the depths of the pain I felt.

There is everything to say and nothing.

I was in agony. Dark fear circulated through my body and mind. Then I went numb. I felt Vida, but little else.

Wade was around sometimes, but not truly Wade anymore. How could he be.

Robin had become a leader. She was persisting, somehow.

I knew how. By helping others.

Wade was going to live elsewhere. There were practical realities. And the realities of sorrow both indescribable and immeasurable.

A man had bought this place. A man I did not know. But he had daughters. Wade made sure of that. That was something. Vida and I would watch over them. There would be girls' laughter rising up among the flowers once again.

Robin left detailed instructions about us. Aspen came to say goodbye. Everyone cried. I stood in place and did not move.

I could not move. I could not escape the pain within these walls.

Vida stood with me. I replayed my time with Lucy over and over in my mind. The monumental. The quiet and delicate. The smallest gifts of kindness shared as glances, words, touch. Her bravery, bold and vibrant, even when it wavered. It always returned. She had always returned.

She was like a forest. Like our forest. Our forest sanctuary, where we were free to explore and observe and wonder, safe from the callous and the indifferent alike. Where everything seemed possible, and we were part of real beauty.

I had Vida. Lucy made sure I had Vida. She honored me. Her love reached beyond death.

We waited, Vida and me. Suns came and went. Moons came and went.

Leon kept the gardens tidy, but no one tended to the pool. No one came to the house. Then Leon stopped coming.

Finally, the sound of engines preannounced an arrival, but we heard cars, not trucks. Two men in suits walked through. They did not notice us. Almost as soon as they arrived, they were gone.

The birds who were still around sang. Smoke hung in the air again, blocking out many days of the sun's rays, but the heat did not relent.

The sound of a louder engine woke us from what became increasingly long slumbers. A truck. Men began unloading furniture around the pool. Red lounge chairs that said "Vista" in white letters. Other men erected Vista signs. The pool was cleaned. People in Vista shirts started arriving.

But no one moved in.

There was no proprietor. There was no family as Wade had intended. There were no little girls who would laugh and dance and read and write and smell the flowers and sing us songs.

I pictured Lucy as a little girl. Her curiosity. Her audacity. Her defiant compassion in the face of injustice, which only grew and expanded as she aged.

I had always deliberately avoided the topic, but as time reached forward, I still knew, deep within my heart, that she would, one day, be gone.

I was not ready for life without Lucy. Maybe I never would have been ready. Some love may be too strong, too deep. There is no preparation sufficient for losing love that transcendent.

Lucy's life, her time, had come to an end. Lucy's light had gone out.

No, Lucy's light had not gone out. I would not let it.

Regardless of what was still to come, her light would keep shining.

Strangers started to come and lounge by the pool, and the music became loud, much of it not very good. Vida and I took leave, initially pausing at the elevated garden, but then moving beyond it so we could settle in a place where we could focus on listening to the birds. A man and a woman arrived behind us with a large wheelbarrow. They strained to hoist me into it and, of course, failed. The man walked off back in the direction of the pool while the woman remained.

"Sorry, kiddos. Need you near the pool. Them's the rules."

I did not know what she meant by any of it. Kiddos? Us? We were two distinguished senior members of this revered facility, nationally recognized for our longevity and tenure. Rules? The last I had heard, the rules here included "do not bother the tortoise[s]."

Multiple men appeared and hoisted me into the wheelbarrow. I felt none of the prior glee and exuberance about being transported in such a manner. They stopped by the pool and tilted the wheelbarrow down, which jolted me forward onto the ground. I was able to withdraw my head and neck in time to avoid injury. I remained inside myself, disgusted with this entire situation. I heard a thud beside me and knew Vida had been forced to endure the same indignity.

"Where did it go?" a voice said in front of us.

"It's feeling shy, I guess."

A knocking sound and sensation. Someone was knocking on me!

Then silence, save for the repetitive and tinny music blasting from the stereo. When, some songs later, I heard Beyoncé, I tentatively emerged. Vida was still inside herself.

People took pictures with us. They stared at their phones. They drank. They swam. They partied, a lot, especially at night but also during the heat of the day. Some stomped on the flowers. Vomited in the bushes. All of these things had happened here before, many times. But this was different. These were strangers. Strangers upon strangers. This entire place was filled with strangers. Strangers are not a problem automatically or necessarily. Every friend is first a stranger. But no one here wanted to be our friend. They took photos, made it look like we were friends, and then moved on.

Vida and I again retreated, this time towards the mimosa trees, only to be re-placed in the wheelbarrow and dumped back by the pool. The next day, and the next, and the next, we attempted to flee but were taken back again and again. Vida felt resignation and thought we should just stay, but I did not want to surrender, and she respected my fervor and militance. For dozens of suns, we set off every morning, then were caught and dumped. The men who trucked us back were rarely the same people. Even the gardeners changed by the week or day.

"Maybe they'll have turtle babies," someone said, posing for a photo beside me. I retreated into myself.

The seriousness of this situation came slowly but surely, then all at once, a devastating realization. We could not escape. We were trapped.

How on earth had this happened?

There was one woman who worked around the pool who was kind to us. She would ask people to take it easy if they tried to touch us and calmly explained that we were sensitive. Thankfully, she reappeared more frequently than most of the other Vista shirts.

On a rare cooler day, she arrived with Dr. Lambeau. Dr. Lambeau! The flood of emotions I felt upon seeing her was overwhelming.

"How are you two beauties doing?" she asked, checking our eyes and mouths with a little light. "Are you giving them any additional food, or are they subsisting on what's growing in the environment—sorry, I've forgotten what your name is. I apologize."

"Austina. I've only been here for about a month, and I haven't seen them being fed. I wasn't told anything about that, and I work in the pool area where they are kept."

"They can go for long periods without eating or drinking if they need to, but there is plenty of food for them around here, the grasses and flowers. Their favorite is fruit, though. You can give them some fruit if you like."

"Okay, thanks. If you could stop by the lobby and tell the manager too, that would be great."

"I will." Dr. Lambeau looked around. "It is a lot busier. They will probably retreat to quieter places. Vida was in a zoo so is used to a fair bit of activity, but I suspect Fernandita may prefer a calmer environment. Although she has been here so long, who knows what she's seen." Dr. Lambeau stood up.

"I saw the name Fernandita on the sign, but which one is she?"

"Vida is the taller one, although she's younger. Fernandita here is one hell of a survivor. Somehow, here she always is."

"I'll get some Destiny's Child playing."

Dr. Lambeau laughed. "And Gloria Gaynor."

Austina nodded, but I could tell she was not certain who that was. I certainly appreciated both song ideas.

"Tortoises cannot regulate their own body temperatures," Dr. Lambeau explained. "They need external sources to make their bodies cool off, like mud or mud puddles, wet soil even. Shade would normally be okay, but on really hot days they should have other options ideally. Can you get them cooled off?"

"Hoses we've got," Austina said. "They don't swim?"

"No, they float but cannot swim. Please keep them well away from the pool's edge for their safety."

Austina nodded. "I'll do my best."

Dr. Lambeau opened a container with two strawberries, which Vida and I happily devoured. People rushed over to film us eating. "It's the best ASMR," one said, which I did not understand.

"Do you oversee these turtles?" one older woman asked.

"They are tortoises actually," Dr. Lambeau replied. "I'm a professor who specializes in reptiles like these but am based in West Virginia. These tortoises are about ninety and one hundred and eighteen years old. There's a plaque about this one over there."

Our doctor was also a professor. How impressive!

"Whoa," one of the people who had been filming us said. "Are you serious?"

"I am."

"That's humbling," the older woman said, and I appreciated both the sentiment and the correct use of the word *humbling*.

Dr. Lambeau nodded. "Sure is."

The people who had been filming us went back to their lounge chairs, and Dr. Lambeau had to leave.

Austina managed to get certain changes put into place as a result of what she had learned. Most significantly, we were no longer forced to remain right beside the pool, but instead were permitted to roam in the adjacent garden areas, provided that we did not venture too far.

"Oh yes, the tortoises are here somewhere."

The Vista-shirted person would look around, see us, and then point. Austina would walk the strangers over herself. They would take pictures, then move on. She was very patient and polite with people, even when they were neither. Sometimes men, including old men, would stare at her when she walked by or away, saying no words, even as their impolite thoughts were obvious.

Vida and I tested the boundaries of what was deemed acceptable. We wanted to know how much was possible for us. Through sustained field research, we determined that we could go in any of the gardens near the plaque or towards the building now formerly known as the residence but not as far as the redbuds and elevated garden or mimosa trees, unfortunately. The Vista shirts preferred we did not even begin to ascend the hill on the mimosa-tree side. That was the way to the forest, to its sanctuary, which felt a world away. When we first tried to move towards it, a group of Vista shirts literally turned us around. They nearly caused me to roll down the hill, but I managed to stay upright due to a spectacularly well-timed placement of my sturdy legs.

It got hotter and hotter. Austina would hose us off when she was working, and bring us fruit. She would always find us, wherever we were, and never turn us around.

The cooler days came later and were not as cool. They did still translate into fewer people being around, and we would take the opportunity to push the boundaries once again. Our strategy was to subtly expand out each day. We slept by the plaque one moon. Then the next day moved to the lady ferns a few tortoise lengths beyond. A little farther along the next day and so on.

Despite having managed to secure more distance, the noise from a rowdy group tore through the air. They did not mind the cooler weather and all but took over the pool area. I tried to ignore their bluster, but there was a lot of it. As the sun descended, their volume ascended.

"This is our time!" one yelled.

"We are back, baby!"

They all cheered. I felt for Austina having to get them drinks and food. The smell of burnt animal flesh mixed with the smoke in the air.

Vida and I settled in among a cluster of thick bushes and tucked into ourselves for slumber. Our ability to block out noise had become well honed.

A profoundly alarming sensation jolted me awake. So many hands. Touching me. Moving me. I was being rocked.

A primal state of panic surged through me.

The movement surged.

Laughter. Awful laughter.

I did not even hiss, for that would have been a pitiful and futile gesture. The laughter subsided.

I could see the lights around the pool. But everything was upside down.

. . .

I moved my legs. I moved them as hard as I could. There was nothing beneath them. No soil, no earth. Time stretched out. The sun returned.

Stress was coursing through Vida. She pushed me. She pushed me again with more force, with all her might. She was trying. She kept trying.

She touched my nose with hers and lay down at my side.

Someone would see me. Someone would walk by. Some new group would arrive and want to take photos. Austina would search until she found us.

Surely someone would care.

It took two more suns for a person to notice me. They took a picture, then left, and returned with Vista shirts who rocked me back upright. Vida and I never saw Austina again.

Hindsight Is 20/20

FEWER VISITOR STRANGERS came. Those who did had become less interested in taking pictures with us, so we were permitted to roam more freely, although this was about their indifference, not our choices or freedom. At first, we avoided the entire pool area like the plague, but there were certain pleasant groups, so Vida and I would go closer to them (but not what I would call close). This was how we learned what was happening outside these walls: People were getting sick.

Vida and I began to roam wherever and whenever we wanted. We would see the occasional person by the pool, but then that stopped and there were not even any Vista shirts around. One man would walk through once or twice a day, sometimes miss a sun, and then reappear. On a particularly strange occasion, ice pellets fell from the sky. But then the heat returned with even deeper intensity.

People slowly began returning. Dr. Lambeau was among the first! Our spirits rose as soon as we saw her walking slowly towards us. She examined our bodies thoroughly and gave us each an entire orange, smiling warmly as we ate, though she seemed tired too.

Signs and loungers were changed from Vista to Premier. Someone from the government was escorted to us by a man in a Premier shirt we had never seen before. The government woman kneeled down, studied us, said we appeared well, then left. I wondered how many other animals she was responsible for monitoring.

Time stretched forward, and the only visitors were those on holiday. On a pleasant and relatively quiet afternoon, a family with two girls caught my attention due to their jovial and easygoing nature. Vida and I watched them from afar before deciding to move closer to enjoy the extra-bubbly sound of the girls' laughter. They noticed me and rushed over but then slowed to a walk as they got closer. Apprehension? Respect? I cannot say. They explained to their parents that I was a tortoise (I believe the adults already knew that but allowed the taller girl to elaborate). Vida cautiously approached, and the pair of us side by side in all our glory caused quite a celebration.

"There's a story on the plaque in the garden behind that cabana," one of the mothers said, pointing. "In 2010, you two weren't even born yet, but one of these tortoises was one hundred and ten years old! Can you believe that?"

The girls' eyes grew large. "Whoa."

"So, if the tortoise was one hundred and ten years old in 2010, how old would that make her today?"

The girls counted on their hands a couple of times and engaged in some deliberation.

"A hundred and twenty-five years old!"

"That's right!"

"She is older than you!"

The mothers laughed.

"You are incredible," the smaller girl said as she got closer. She studied me. "May I please touch her?"

The parents looked at each other, and the one mother shrugged.

"I think you can try, but pay attention to what she does," the other mother said. "If she pulls back, it means she would prefer you didn't touch her. That would be her saying, 'No, thank you.'"

"She can't talk!" the little girl said.

"She can, in her own way. You have to pay attention."

The little girl reached her hand forward, and I booped it with my nose. She laughed and pulled her hand back. Then she reached it out again and gingerly touched my neck, her smile beaming. The taller sister stretched towards Vida, who also happily received the gentle touch. It was delightful. I felt fifty again.

In fact, I felt more hopeful than I had in quite some time, though cautiously so. Children like this raised by mothers (and/or fathers) like this had little lights within them. I could feel the weight placed on them, the grip squeezing their lungs, but they breathed deeply somehow, nonetheless. It was as though they carried with them the strength of all the girls who had come before, who had fiercely or tentatively become women. These girls were carrying pain but also possibility. At times, they had to drag the latter along, while in other moments it propelled them. I knew exactly how that felt.

I thought of Jasmine and wondered who she would have become. She would have been perfect, whatever she chose.

The thoughtful visitors brought us great joy, but unfortunately, there were more impolite groups than kind ones. One girl and her brother took turns tossing empty cans at me, which was certifiably rude, and Vida and I took leave without delay. There were parties, even the occasional proper social gathering. There was a book launch with lovely people. I hoped Robin or Aspen might appear, but sadly, they did not. I understood the many reasons why, the practical as well as the emotional.

There was a brilliant party for a company making meat without animals. That was most intriguing albeit also somewhat confusing. Chickens were being held together in large groups indoors, thousands of them at a time or more, where dangerous sicknesses can spread quickly among birds and to people. It sounded absolutely dreadful. I immediately thought of Peace and Freedom, and their gentle, curious minds. During the mingling portion of the evening, one woman got very emotional and said they were going to change the world. Her devotion glowed like the sun.

I hoped there were many more people like this, filled with kindness and compassion. My hope was stubborn.

Dr. Lambeau returned! Oh, it was a jubilant occasion despite the even deeper markers of time on her face, lines commemorating laughter and anger alike. She greeted us with worthy compliments and mango.

A boy came over and stood nearby with his mother.

"Are you checking on the tortoises?" the mother asked, and Dr. Lambeau nodded. "He loves animals."

"Come on over, and I'll teach you about these two incredible individuals. This one is Vida, and this one, her name is Fernandita, but you can call her Fern for short."

"Fern! Like in *Charlotte's Web*!" the boy said.

Dr. Lambeau smiled. "That's right."

The boy sat down on the ground and watched as Dr. Lambeau inspected our bodies. She narrated her work, and he listened intently to every word, properly understanding probably half of it but keen nevertheless.

I felt a sharp poke in my shoulder. Mercifully, the sensation disappeared just as quickly as it had appeared.

"Sorry about that, baby girl," Dr. Lambeau said, rubbing my neck and offering me another slice of mango. She gave some to the boy, and he gently handed it to Vida with determined focus.

Dr. Lambeau began to pack up her medical items.

"Thank you very much for this lesson," the boy said. "I learned a lot."

"You are very welcome. It was my pleasure. This might even have been the start of something remarkable."

The boy looked uncertain but curious. I expect I did too.

"It's early, so I don't want to get ahead of things, but we're going to try and revive the Fernandinas."

All members of this little audience, human and tortoise alike, were confused.

"Some of my colleagues were able to extract a sample from a tortoise whose life ended a long time ago but whose remains are only a few hours from here, actually. He might've been brought over on the same ship as Fern. We may be able to combine his sample with DNA from this young lady right here and work some scientific magic." She rubbed my neck and held up the vial of blood. Of my blood.

The boy looked at her quizzically, but his mother smiled. "Do you mean you might be able to basically bring the tortoises back who were all gone?" she asked.

"That's right, more or less. The Fernandina species was thought to be extinct until we found this beauty right here. We might be able to create more of her kind now."

"Wow."

The boy did not fully understand, but was smiling, sensing everyone's excitement.

"This gentle giant"—Dr. Lambeau nodded to Vida—"the Aldabra, her species lived in Madagascar and then the Seychelles islands in Africa. There were giant tortoises in most parts of the world at some point. It's looking like we'll be able to reintroduce many of her kind to Madagascar very soon, only six hundred years later."

"Are you serious?" the mother asked.

"Absolutely. We can't turn back time, but we can try to make amends." Dr. Lambeau looked at the child. "So, remember, keep being curious. But most importantly, keep caring."

I breathed in these words, every one of them, and emanated joy.

Resolute

BUT PEOPLE GOT sick again. There were no visitors, kind or otherwise, and no updates about tortoises beyond these walls. Vida and I spent an extended period of time near what had been the swans' pond, trying to keep cool. The summers were filled with smoke, and at some point, even autumn was.

People eventually came back, but far fewer of them. They were rowdy, but there was an indifference about them too, a fog of resignation as thick as smoke. We observed the human part of the place but kept our distance. Dr. Lambeau did not come back, and my heart ached.

Nothing changed and then it did. People got sick yet again. The sense of terror was hard to describe. That was definitively the most afraid people have ever been in this place.

Then they vanished.

Men who were certainly not sanctioned guests came and took things from inside the residence. We retreated promptly to the swans' former pond. It was half the size it had been. There were no frogs left at all. We hid among the bushes.

No people came back.

Vida and I had free rein of the whole place. Everywhere we went, we went together. I moved around more quickly than Vida, despite being older than her, so slowed my pace to match hers. I investigated the front gate, while she dozed close by. I rejoined her promptly, but we did not move off right away. Why would we. There was little to avoid and even less to pursue.

There were no birds. No bees. No mammals of any kind. I could not properly understand why we were the only ones who remained.

A thousand smoky suns passed. We governed our movements based on how we felt, what we wanted to eat, and where we could find some reprieve from the heat (or falling ice spears when those returned). We rested in the shade under the memorial oak trees, and near the garden planted in honor of Jasmine, the living roots and branches of Lucy's life. We spent a lot of time near the graves. Vida felt the animals through me, as vibrant memories of them danced in my heart. Some with names, others I knew by their songs. My chosen family.

How I missed music.

I would not have been able to accept—not accept, but endure—its absence without Vida.

Then, one morning, Vida did not emerge from within herself. I approached her and felt it.

Her absence.

Vida was gone. I was alone.

Time gives and takes everything. Everyone.

Everyone I have ever loved is gone.

Time stretches forward unrelentingly. Unapologetically. I believe I am 150 years of age.

I am a tortoise. I am proud to be a tortoise. I am also a prism. The gleaming rays of light, shimmering, precise as petals, I share them.

There were always people trying to guide others towards an uneven but more humane path. To care for the soil. To sustain the gardens, and nurture new ones with gentle and mighty care, sometimes boldly, often quietly.

Branches have reached farther than ever before, and new hardy plants have emerged, some rising up through cracks in the concrete. The beauty is sublime. I am interconnected with this place. I have remained devoted through all its changing states and statuses. Still, a longing for my homeland floats through like mist. I wonder whether any of my relatives are there, my descendants; if I helped people to make amends, and to atone. Sometimes I imagine that I am welcomed into its symphony, as a harp or maybe simply as a chime.

I am here, and hope lives in me.

I have seen three birds, two blue, one black and red. They did not sing, though they may still. I truly believe they are harbingers.

Because at first, I thought I was dreaming. But somewhere beyond these walls, I heard it. A chorus.

"Stayin' alive, stayin' alive."

There are two gates. I am going to check them both.

Acknowledgments

IT WAS A profound joy writing this novel. I feel such gratitude to those who helped bring the tortoise to the world that it's difficult to gather words that are worthy, but I offer this bouquet.

My agent, Chris Bucci, a veritable wizard who can make even the wildest dreams come true, guided this story (and its author) with steadfast commitment and vision to a superb home at Simon & Schuster. He may well be as good a man as Nikki thinks he is.

The brilliance of editor extraordinaire Olivia Taylor Smith dazzles, even more so because it is matched by a generosity of heart that stretches around the globe. I am infinitely thankful to you for believing in Magic. You have now saved two Monkeys and make the world a kinder place in many ways.

To Brittany Adames, expansive thanks for the thoughtfulness and skill you brought to this book at every stage of the process. Nicole Brugger-Dethmers understood the deeper hopes nestled in these chapters and treated them with nuanced care through her intricate copyediting work. Thank you to Danielle Prielipp, Shannon Hennessey, Martha Langford, Amanda Mulholland, Olivia Perrault, Lauren Gomez, Morgan Hart, Ruth Lee-Mui, Allyson Floridia, Chelsey Drysdale, Bryn McDonald, Meryll Preposi, Beth Maglione, Samantha Cohen, Mikaela Bielawski, Math Monahan, Jackie Seow, Emma Shaw, Tom Spain, Ray Chokov, Nicole Moran, Michael Nardullo, Mabel Taveras, Lyndsay Brueggemann, Winona

Lukito, Tim O'Connell, Irene Kheradi, and Sean Manning for treating the tortoise and her tale so well.

The mighty and savvy team at Simon & Schuster Canada, led by the formidable Nicole Winstanley, is a national treasure. I am deeply grateful to you all and especially to Natasha Kempnich, Maya Price-Baker, and my wonderful editor Brittany Lavery, whose insights on this novel and those within it made my spirit sing. Thank you for your wisdom and even more so for your kindness.

The first reader of this book, Amy Jones, offered an ocean's worth of support and brings such genuine care to the waterways and shores of words. Jen, Gord, Martha: Heartfelt thanks for being incredible humans and early readers. The enthusiasm fellow 519er Laurie Elizabeth Flynn shares with authors, including this one, demonstrates the very best of literary community.

My mother helped me meet and respect animals on pages and in person even before I could walk, and I wish all children experienced such opportunities and their lifelong impacts. I'm also thankful for the friends who understand just how much writing means to me.

I love working at Huron University College at Western University and appreciate supportive leaders, colleagues, coworkers, and students. Special thanks to endlessly helpful Katherine Mazur-Spitzig and the timeless passion of the Huron Literary Society.

I am grateful to Dr. Sawako Akai, who generously helped with the Japanese phrases. Chi miigwech to Mary Lou Smoke and Dr. Christy Bressette, phenomenal Indigenous women leaders with whom I spoke about my desire to respectfully include the Anishinabek Creation Story in this novel and honor Anishinaabe people as an ally.

Those who defend and champion sentient beings of all kinds, from dogs, horses, and donkeys to chickens, gorillas, and frogs, are a primary reason my own hope is stubborn. The real world of tortoise protection reaches from the Galápagos Islands to Madagascar and beyond. Conservation and wildlife rehabilitation rooted in respect for multispecies communities and animals' individual and collective lives—including those who are not endangered—not only inspire me as a novelist, but also as a grateful resident on this precious yet vulnerable planet, our only home. Jonathan and Fernanda are whole symphonies. It is my greatest hope that this novel helps our species to make amends and genuinely respect animals, including their relatives—what I think they would want most.

To the songwriters, novelists, screenwriters, playwrights, poets, and authors of all kinds who share challenging and perspicacious shades and shimmers: my solidarity and thanks. To readers, booksellers, librarians, and all those who understand the transformative power of creativity and welcome the tortoise into your hearts: a giant thank you. To everyone who dares to imagine or seeks to understand the feelings of animals and fervently cultivates empathy: Please don't ever stop.

Zella, Kozzie, Henry, Zeke, Sunny, Buster, Ms. Macey, Trooper, Quinn, Aquila, Sarge, Sophie . . . pure love.

John: All the words in the universe couldn't even begin to properly reflect the gratitude I feel for you and your ever-expanding love and support. You help make everything possible.

Keep singing.

About the Author

KENDRA COULTER earned her PhD at the University of Toronto and is a Professor at Huron University College at Western University, where she leads the world's first major in animal ethics and sustainability leadership. She is a Fellow of the Oxford Centre for Animal Ethics in England and the author of *Defending Animals: Finding Hope on the Front Lines of Animal Protection*. *The Tortoise's Tale* is her first novel.